The Archaic Chest

12 Tales of Shadow

Kristina Orlea

This is a work of fiction. Names, characters, businesses, government land, and events are products of the author's imagination or internet research to be used in a fictitious manner.

Any resemblance to actual persons, living or dead, is purely coincidental.

First Edition

Published by Sleepless Sanctuary Publishing 2022

www.thenosleeppodcast.com

ISBN: 9798836227197

Cover Illustration: Gemma Amor

As I lay here dying

In my personal oubliette

The thing I miss the most

Is the blood red sunset…

Table of Contents

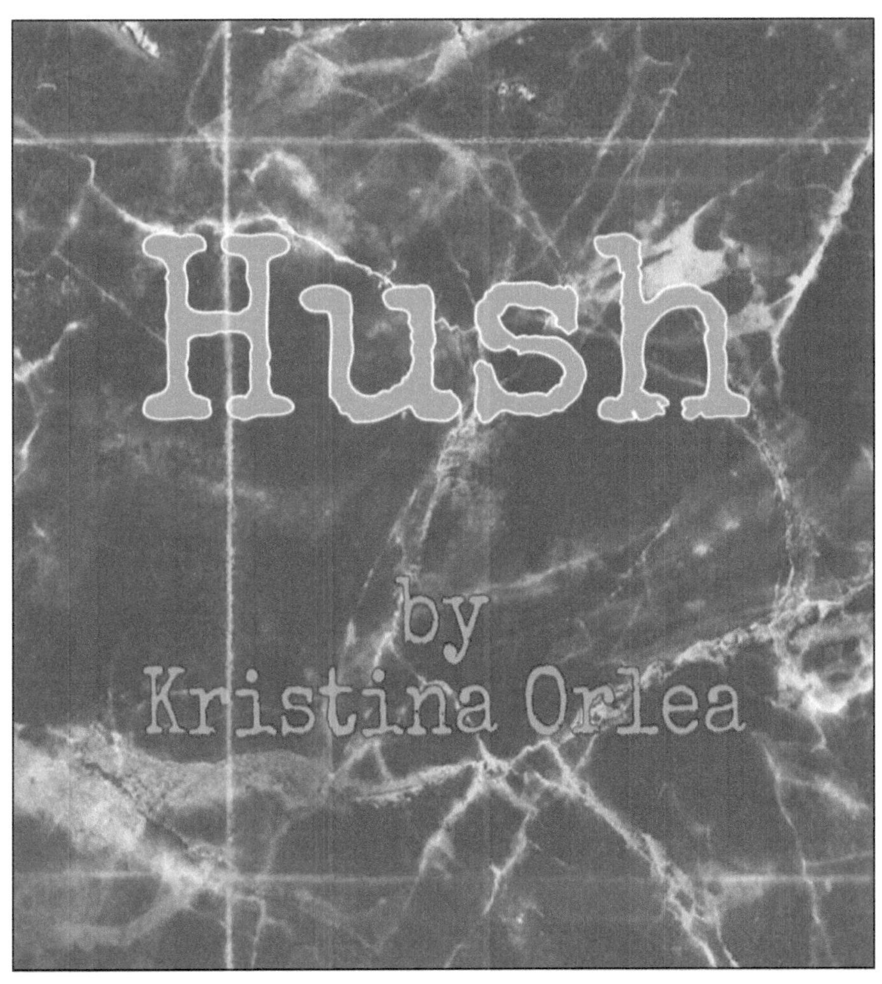

In the dark, no words can escape…

Hush

I was out doing some much-needed food shopping; work and life had gotten extremely busy, and I had completely forgotten that I was out of… well, pretty much everything. I had just grabbed a bottle of shampoo and tossed it into my trolley when my mobile buzzed twice from my back pocket.

Pulling my phone out, I saw that I had two new emails about a work project. Longing for a quiet shopping experience, I tapped the dismiss button and pushed my trolley towards the next aisle. I had taken four steps when I looked up just in nick of time to keep from ramming into an overly large and obnoxious display of men's razors set up in the middle of the aisle. Mortified, I looked around to see if anyone had witnessed my fumble. It was still early in the day, and most people were still at work, so it appeared that my awkward moment was private. I put my mobile in my back pocket and steered the trolley away from the razor display. That's when I saw her peering out of an aisle. My embarrassing moment had a witness.

I couldn't quite make out her features; she stood roughly my height, she wore a red dress, white gloves, and a black scarf across her mouth and nose. She just stood there, staring at me. It was rather creepy, and I was already unnerved from my near miss collision with the unpleasant razor display, so I just smiled, dropped my head, and kept walking.

I made my way through the rest of the store, grabbing everything on the list, including a few extras. I had just finished shopping and was turning my trolley to head to the front when I caught a glimpse of the woman from earlier standing at the end of the bread aisle, staring at me. I turned to get a better look, but she was gone. Not wanting to draw attention to myself, I quickly checked out, loaded the groceries, and headed right home.

***

After a few days, I'd completely forgotten about the strange woman in the supermarket. A week later, I was out doing some chores, one of which involved picking up some screws to reinforce an old writing table that had begun to wobble. I was in the DIY store trying to figure out which type of wood screw I needed when I had this strange sensation that I was being watched. I figured it was just the clerk checking on me; I'd been standing there glaring at screws for quite a while, so I looked up and smiled but there wasn't anyone near. There was, however, a weird woman across the road, peering at me through the large store display window. I immediately recognized her as the woman from the market; she was even wearing the same clothes.

I squinted as I looked out the window. "What the fuck?"

"Sorry?" a young man's voice spoke up from behind me.

I swiftly turned around to see the shop clerk looking at me curiously. "Oh, uh, sorry 'bout that, mate. I just thought I saw someone." I twisted towards the window to show him what I was referring to, but the woman was gone.

From that day on, I started seeing the creepy woman every other day; on my way to the shops, to work, even to the gym. She was never close, always just far enough away that all I could make out was the red dress and black scarf, but it was her. Every time I felt the hair on the back of my neck stand on end, I knew she was there watching me. She seemed to be everywhere.

***

Every other day quickly became every day. I felt like I was going mad; I would catch just a glimpse of her. Only a glimpse. I can't quite explain it, but it was like each time I saw her, she was slowly coming more into view. I was able to make out more of her physical features. The dress was raggedy; it looked to be an old paisley pattern, with reds and whites, that at one time I'm sure was quite cute but now was tattered and frayed. At one time I might have owned something similar, I'm not certain, but it felt familiar. The gloves covering her hands were a dingy white and looked loose on her fingers, like they were a size too big. Her hair was wild and stringy, like she was always caught in a heavy windstorm. It was always obscuring most of her face, leaving only the black scarf visible.

The scarf. The most disturbing part. It was the only part of clothing that was ever vibrant in color. The fabric looked silky smooth with a hint of shimmer that made it stand out in a crowd. It covered her mouth and nose so that between the shimmery fabric and her hair, you couldn't see any of her facial features.

I'm not going lie, I was getting increasingly ticked off and more than just a little creeped out by her constant presence. I mean, what the bloody hell did this lady want from me? How and why was she following me everywhere? Did she know me? Did I do something to her?

I wasn't sure I wanted to find out.

***

One gloomy Saturday, a month after the DIY sighting, I was walking past Yeats Cemetery on my way to the library when I saw her again. She was on the other side of the stone fence, standing next to a large oak tree and gazing in my direction. This time she was much closer to me, close enough to confront. And I decided I needed to put an end to this one way or another.

"Hey!" I hollered out as I clambered over the fence.

She just stood there. As I approached her, I got this weird sensation of familiarity; growing stronger the closer I got.

"Who are you? Why are you following me?" I demanded.

She neither spoke nor moved. She just simply stared at me. I kept walking. When I was roughly ten feet from her, she stepped away from the tree, in my direction. Her features were completely visible to me now. Her hair was a dull, wiry grey that hung in her face. She had sad, deep-set eyes that pierced through the hair and stabbed right through me. My scalp tingled as that feeling increased and, reluctantly, I stepped a little closer.

Once I was right in front of her, I realized what was causing the sensation. It was as if I was looking into a mirror, a mirror that had somehow aged me seventy years. Completely bewildered and extremely irritated that this woman, who somehow resembled me, wasn't answering my very pointed questions, I stepped closer.

"I asked you a question." My voice trembled from equal parts anger and fear.

She just stared right through me, not speaking a word. My fear was overcome by anger, and I reached out for her scarf. Her eyes changed from melancholy to curious, but she didn't pull away. I grabbed ahold of the scarf and tugged. My eyes followed as it left my hand and floated down to the ground, then I looked up at her and immediately wished I hadn't. The woman's complexion was a vaporous pale gray, and where her mouth should have been, there was nothing. Nothing but stretched, taut, translucent skin.

Terror boiled inside of me and as I opened my own mouth to release the wild scream raging deep in my bowels, the woman cocked her head to the side and took a half step closer. Her eyes became feral and glowed with a carnage I had never witnessed; in one swift, fluid motion, she raised a gloved hand, placed her index finger up to her mouthless face and spoke.

"Hush."

***

My scream never left my lips. Nothing will ever again.

What was once a treasure may just be your fate…

The Archaic Chest

It was a hot, sticky Thursday afternoon. The sun burned bright in the sky as three women sat drinking mimosas on the patio of 'The Bistro on Elm'. Sarah motioned for the waitress to bring another round.

"Alright, Nancy. I'm dying to know all about you. Tell me everything!"

Sarah emptied her glass and nodded in agreement with Kelly. "Yes, please do. What brings you to our little town?"

Nancy took a sip and smiled. "Well, I'm a freelance interior designer, formerly based out of Baton Rouge. I moved to Hammond to get away from the noise of the city."

The waitress placed three new mimosas on the table, cleared the empty glasses, and left the check. Sarah and Kelly both reached for it, but Nancy snatched it up.

"Oh, and I like long walks on the beach, sunsets, and I'm a sucker for beignets." She placed cash on the table. "Anything else?"

Kelly giggled.

Sarah raised her glass. "Here's to new friendships and cold mimosas!"

The women toasted each other and laughed.

Nancy then pointed across the street. "Oh, I love antiques shops! Have either of you been there?"

Confused, Sarah and Kelly looked at each other, then over at the building Nancy was pointing at.

“Maybe it’s the mimosas but I don’t remember that shop being there,” Sarah said.

“Oh, it must be new! I remember hearing about a new shop opening.” Kelly grabbed her purse and stood up. “We should go check it out.”

The three of them walked across the street and as they approached the shop, Sarah felt a chill, cold enough to create goose bumps across her neck and arms. As she looked up at the seemingly ancient sign, she got a slight case of vertigo. Shifting slightly, she reached out to grab Kelly’s arm to sturdy herself, but the moment they touched the feeling was gone.

“Sarah, are you alright?” Nancy asked.

“I’m good, I think that I might’ve had one too many mimosas.” She giggled. “And I think they’re catching up to me.”.

The inside of the store was laid out like most antique stores; a room containing bookshelves that held tattered and torn leather-bound books, chairs that had seen better days, hutches filled with chipped china, lamps made of ornate glass, dressers topped with old photographs, racks of clothes; the smell was a mix of mothballs, moldy leather, and musty aged fabric. It was an oddly welcoming scent.

Being an avid reader, Sarah immediately turned in the direction of the bookshelves. Kelly, the town’s fashionista, always looking for new trends or trying to bring back old ones, veered off towards the clothing racks. Nancy didn’t have an immediate response to any of the items, so she just wondered off towards the furniture.

There were several tall bookshelves, each over-flowing with books, magazines, and newspapers. Among them were titles that Sarah recognized; “War of the Worlds”, “Mutiny on the Bounty”, “Treasure Island”, “Catcher and the Rye”; mixed in were titles that she had never heard of, let alone could pronounce. One title caught her eye, “*Annulum de Daemonium*", she had absolutely no clue what that translated to, but she couldn't stop looking at it. Entranced by the binding, she picked the book up. It smelled of old paper, roses, and tobacco. As she held it affectionately, she noticed that the crimson red leather bounding was smooth, bare of any scratch marks, and yet the title appeared chiseled, and the letters shimmered like black glittery ink.

As she was about to open the book, Kelly squealed from somewhere in the middle of the store. Snapping out of her trance, Sarah grabbed up a few other books she had set aside and hurried over to see what had Kelly excited.

Sarah rounded the corner and saw Kelly over by a clothing rack, holding a gorgeous ruby red dress and jumping up and down like an enthusiastic child on Christmas morning. Apparently, her excitement caught Nancy's attention as well, because she came out from the furniture section holding a beautiful stained-glass table lamp.

Before either of them could speak, Kelly started rambling on about the dress.

"I've been looking for one just like this forever and wouldn't you believe it, Sarah, it's in my size!" Excited was an understatement, she looked at Sarah with eyes wide full of delight. "It's a 1940s swing dress. Since the release of Cate Blanchett's new film, they're coming back in style. I have been dying to get my hands on one!"

Kelly then began to incessantly speed talk about how she had the perfect pair of Michael Kors heels and the most adorable Louis Vuitton glitter clutch that would both pair perfectly with the dress. As she was admiring the dress in the mirror, Sarah noticed the lamp that Nancy was holding. Pointing at the lamp, she asked Nancy what she had found.

Nancy blushed. "I found what I believe might be a rare Tiffany Dragonfly table lamp. These things should sell for $25,000!" She pointed out the markings on the bottom. "And with a tag price of $120, I couldn't pass it up."

Sarah looked blankly at the lamp and shrugged.

"Rare or not, I'm gonna buy it. It's beautiful and my apartment could use some light." She nodded to the stack of books Sarah was holding and smiled. "A bit of light reading?"

Looking at the books in her arms, Sarah asked, "Has anyone seen the shop keeper?"

As if summoned, a stout old woman popped out from behind a cabinet and greeted them.

"Sorry 'ta keep you ladies waiting. I'm not as agile as I once was," the woman chimed. She spread her arms out. "Welcome to The Archaic Chest, I see that each of you have found something special. Now let's get you ringed up."

She turned and pointed to a trinket filled counter holding an old-fashioned cash register and started walking that way. The three women looked at each other, shrugged and followed the woman. Once at the counter, they could make out the features of the woman. She was not tall, but she also wasn't short, it was as if her size was in flux. She had long silvery hair that flowed around her face like water, there was barely a wrinkle on her tawny beige skin and her voice was melodic with an accent they couldn't quite place. This woman was unusual indeed.

Kelly was the first to the counter, she carefully placed the dress on the glass top and the old woman smiled.

"Oh my, you found my favorite dress! I acquired 'dis dress at Cinéma du Panthéon, a small theatre just outside of Baton Rouge. They were in the middle of renovations a few years back, and they found all sorts of treasures. Would you believe dat this beauty was found in a closet?"

She clicked a few buttons on the register and placed the dress in a brown paper bag. “Well, no one had claimed the dress, nor could anyone think of who it could’ve belonged to. So, dey gave me a call and I brought it here,” she grinned. “And today, you get it for $80.00.”

Kelly paid the woman and stepped to the side. Nancy placed the lamp on the counter and the woman locked eyes with her and beamed with nostalgia.

“Ah, now dis, dis lamp was found in the beautiful LeDoux manor, in the out skirts of New Orleans. Thibodaux, I do believe. Just before it ‘twas to be demolished. Such a shame that was. Such a shame.”

Nancy gave the woman her credit card and she rang it up.

Sarah stood just behind Nancy and the woman noticed she was holding a stack of books. Pointing to the book bound in red leather her expression changed from cheerful to that of melancholy.

“Now dat, dat is also from LeDoux Manor. It was rumored dat the head maid, Chantale, a Haitian woman, and Madam LeDoux were lovers. Folks didn’t take to that very well, said that the maid must have bewitched the madam. After many years of speculation, harassment, shunnin’, and the like, the family just up and disappeared. Left almost all their belongin’s behind and not ta word as to where ‘dey went.” She looked up at the women. “Madam LeDoux’s brother was the one to discover ‘da empty house. He was a priest that traveled from parish to parish to assist with this and that, and he would stay at the manor from time to time. I believe most of the books were his, apparently didn’t want nothing that had been close to witchcraft.” She placed the books in a brown paper bag.

The woman politely thanked them for their purchases, and they walked out of the store. As Sarah passed through the doorway, she felt the chill from earlier. As soon as they were on the street, it was gone.

Nancy glanced down at her watch, "Shit! It's going on four and I have a Skype meeting with a new client at five. Thanks for the lovely afternoon, ladies, but I do need to get going."

"See you Saturday morning at hot yoga!" Kelly chimed.

"Oh, I hope my back is recovered by then," Sarah said.

They said their goodbyes and each of them went their separate ways.

***

Once Sarah got home, she poured a glass of wine and got comfortable on the sofa. She emptied the bag of books on to the coffee table and immediately picked up the red book, examining the outside of it; it was smooth to the touch and seemed to tingle beneath her fingertips. The title, "*Annulum de Daemonium*", was on the front cover in an ink unlike any she had ever seen before. It twinkled in the sunlight and yet blended into the crimson leather like it was part of the material.

She opened the book to the title page; the paper was soft parchment with a hint of marbling. There was the title in bold black letters with the name *Countess LeDoux* in the place where you would expect to find the author's name. As she flipped through the book, admiring the earthy scent, she felt a bulge in the pages. Quickly she flipped through to locate what was creating the bump. Between pages LXXV and LXXVI was a thin, silver ring. Sarah picked it up to examine it. It was simple in design, no stones, just a small vining filigree on the outside of the band. Without thinking, she slid it onto her right ring finger; it fit like a glove.

She admired it on her finger. The silver complimented her warm brown skin. It must have been stashed in the book by someone. It looked old and new all at the same time. She went to take it off, but it wouldn't budge. "Damn. It's stuck."

Putting the book down, she went into the kitchen. She lathered her hand in dish soap and ran it under cool water. No luck. “Well, shit.”

Her stomach gurgled and she realized she was getting hungry. Looking down at her watch she realized that four hours had passed since she had gotten home.

“Damn, where’d the time go?”

She warmed up left-over chicken fried rice and then went back out to the living room. She grabbed the open book that she left on the sofa and put it on the coffee table with the other books.

She turned on the TV, found a show to watch and ate the rice. After an hour, she began to feel tired. She turned off the TV, put her dishes in the kitchen sink and headed to her bedroom. As she was getting undressed, she noticed a small rash on her right wrist.

“Huh, I must have brushed up against something in the antique store,” she mused. Not giving it a second thought, she grabbed her clothes and headed for the shower.

In the living room, the crimson red leather book slowly opened, and a black mist furled out from the pages.

***

Kelly had been the most excited to get home. After all, finding that dress had been the discovery of the year for her. As soon as she got in, she ran straight to her bedroom and laid the dress out on her bed to smooth the wrinkles. Popping out to the kitchen to get a glass of wine, she noticed her cat was acting strange.

The cat paced in front of her bedroom door but wouldn’t enter. “Peppers, sweetie, what are you doing?”

The cat just let out a low hiss and continued to pace.

“I knew I should have gotten you fixed,” Kelly responded. She poured the wine and headed for the bedroom to try on her new favorite dress.

It fit like it was made just for her. Standing in front of the mirror, she swung back and forth, getting the full effect of the swing. The fabric hugged her in all the right places; the neckline made her cleavage pop, and her honey blonde hair was stunning against the ruby color of the dress.

“I can’t believe it, this looks amazing!” She twirled in front of the mirror. “I look amazing! Now let’s see if the shoes match.” She pranced into the closet and pulled a box of shoes off the shelf. “They’re a perfect match!”

As she was putting the high heels back in the box, a blur ran past the bottom of the mirror. She figured it was Peppers finally coming into the room and turned off the closet light.

“I can’t wait to wear this tomorrow! Though I should probably steam it first.” Kelly removed the dress, hung it on a hanger and walked it to the steamer. Setting the dial for Wrinkle Release/Steam she headed off to take a shower. “It’ll be like new in the morning!”

Once out of the shower, she went to put on her pajamas. “That’s odd, these weren’t loose on me this morning.” As she pulled at her shorts, they were slightly baggy. She re-tied the pull string and hopped on the scale. “Oh wonderful, I’m down a pound! That new diet must be working, those five pounds will be gone in no time!” She cheered as she climbed into bed.

***

The next morning, Kelly awoke feeling a bit groggy. It was like she wasn’t quite awake yet. Peppers was laying in her spot on the bed, softly purring.

"I see you got over whatever had you upset last night."

She got out of bed and began her morning routine, which consisted of two cups of coffee paired with a plain English muffin followed by thirty minutes of reading *Fashion Beat Daily*. After some cuddle time with Peppers, to make up for last night, Kelly pulled the dress out of the steamer and went to put it on.

The dress looked even better after being steamed. "It fits me so well." She beamed.

Peppers hissed and ran for the bedroom as Kelly grabbed a white knit sweater from the hallway. She put it on and found it slightly bigger than she remembered.

"Huh. Here's to fad diets!"

***

Sarah awoke to her right arm itching like crazy. The rash, small last night, was now bigger, red, and irritated.

"Man, I must be having a reaction to something. What the hell could I have gotten into?"

She got up, did her morning exercises, cleaned up and got dressed. She found a tube of hydrocortisone cream in the cupboard and lathered the rash in a thick layer, then got ready to head out to run some errands. As she grabbed her bag to leave, she noticed that the red book was open on the coffee table and a thought occurred to her.

Maybe I'm allergic to the paper? It did look like it was made of something other than regular pulp. Running a bit behind, she made a mental note to look at it later, grabbed her keys and left the apartment.

***

After she was done running around town, Sarah met Kelly for a late lunch.

"Oh damn, that looks amazing on you!" Sarah exclaimed when she saw Kelly.

"It does, doesn't it?" Kelly giggled as she spun in a circle to show off the swing of the dress. "I was so afraid that the size would be off, but it fits like a dream."

They sat down and placed their order. As the drinks were coming to the table, Kelly pointed at Sarah's right hand.

"That's new. And it's beautiful, let me see it!"

Confused, Sarah looked down at her wrist, thinking that Kelly had noticed the rash, but then she remembered the ring. Holding out her right hand to show off the silver ring, Sarah explained, "It was inside one of the books I bought. Someone must have stashed it."

"Oh, that's lovely! And it looks so pretty on your hand" Kelly said.

"Yes, I do like it quite a bit. It's just a shame that I got into something that caused this nasty looking rash though." She gestured towards her wrist. "It's starting to get annoying."

Kelly looked at Sarah's arm, up at her face, then down at her arm again. "I don't see any rash, sweetie. Are you sure it hasn't already healed?"

Sarah looked down at the spot on her wrist and sure enough, there was still a nasty looking rash. In fact, it had spread halfway up her forearm since this morning. But the look on Kelly's face was puzzled but honest.

"Oh, well. I guess it's getting better," Sarah muttered as she looked closer at her arm.

As they ate their lunch, Kelly couldn't stop talking about the dress and the results she was getting from her diet. Sarah, on the other hand, was fixated on her arm. They carried on for a bit, neither one really listening to the other, and then it was time for them to head out.

After they paid the server, Kelly stood to put on her sweater. "This damn thing must have gotten stuck on the chair; it feels stretched out."

Sure enough, as she went to put the sweater on, it looked like it was two sizes too big. Sarah had seen Kelly wear that sweater before and it always fit her nicely. It's a shame it might be ruined.

"This looked fabulous this morning! But now look at it!" Kelly sobbed.

Sarah went to console her, but her arm felt weird. She looked down at it and what she saw made her cringe. The rash had turned a dark purplish red and had black lines radiating from the center. It was warm to the touch, and she could've sworn she saw the flesh move. She didn't even speak, she just grabbed her things and bolted for the door.

Kelly called after her, but she didn't stop. Sarah was gone.

Pulling her cell phone out, Kelly tried calling Sarah, but it went straight to voicemail.

"Hey sweetie, I'm not sure what just happened but let me know if you need anything." She grabbed her purse and left the restaurant.

***

Keeping with her Friday ritual, Kelly headed to the local boutique to see what new fashion pieces had arrived. As usual, Clare greeted her as she walked in.

"Is that a new dress? It's remarkable!" Clare fawned.

Kelly did her best catwalk twirl. "I know, isn't it just gorgeous? I couldn't believe it fit without a single alteration."

Clare looked her up and down. "It's like it was sewn just to fit your body. Damn, you are lucky. Speaking of, you've lost weight. You look three sizes smaller. What gives?"

"What are you talking about? I'm the same size I was when I was in here last week. Minus a pound or two."

"No way. Here." She grabbed a size six dress off the rack and handed it to Kelly. "Try this on."

Kelly took the dress and headed for the changing room. Once inside, she tried to unzip the swing dress, but the zipper was stuck. She tried it again, but it wouldn't budge. "Clare, can you help? The zipper is stuck."

"Sure thing." Clare opened the fitting room door to see Kelly struggling with the zipper. "Here, let me try." She gave the zipper a gentle wiggle, but it wouldn't budge for her either. "I don't want to break it. Maybe you can try some bar soap at home."

Kelly nodded. "That was a cute dress you wanted me to try on by the way. Maybe next time."

"Anytime. Though, it may be the lighting, but you do look a few sizes smaller. Won't you tell me your prized weight loss secret?"

"Oh, you're seeing things!" She playfully slapped at Clare. "I just started one of those new Hollywood diets the other day. I want to lose five pounds but there's no way I've lost that much yet." Kelly placed her hands on her hips. "The dress just accents my curves."

She looked at the clock on the far wall, five thirty, Pete was coming by at eight, so she needed to get home. "I'll see you next week!"

***

It took Sarah half an hour to get home. Once there, she stripped off her top shirt and inspected the rash. It covered her entire right arm up to her shoulder and had spread down her arm pit and onto her breast.

In shock, Sarah ran to the full-length mirror so she could get a better look. The outbreak was hideous, purples and reds mixed in with her disfigured flesh. There were boils in various spots and a few had begun to seep a black viscous pus. And the smell, oh God, the smell; a mix of rotting flesh, sewage, and sulfur. If it weren't for her gagging at the putrid smell, she would have screamed out in disgust.

She felt hot and dizzy. Looking at her face in the mirror, she could see the rash was climbing up her neck and was beginning to crest her chin. In the reflection, she could see the red leather book on the coffee table, still open but now there was black vapor twirling out from it. Totally overwhelmed, she screamed, then blacked out.

***

Kelly got to her apartment around six fifteen. She checked the mailbox, grabbed the paper, and went inside. Peppers was asleep in the window. The moment she saw Kelly, she let out a low growl.

"Stupid cat. What's the matter with you?"

Setting the mail and her purse on the counter, Kelly began to tidy up the kitchen. After she was done, she went to freshen herself up. Once in the bedroom, she attempted to unzip the dress again.

"Ugh, still stuck. What did Clare suggest? Oh yeah, bar soap" she muttered as she went to the bathroom. She grabbed a bar from the shower.

She rubbed the soap along the zipper, delicately jiggled it back and forth, then it finally broke loose. "Got it!"

Now unzipped, Kelly was able to remove the dress. She turned and tossed it on the bed. As she did, she caught a quick glimpse of herself in the mirror. Turning to fully face the mirror, she stood horrified. Where she was once firm and toned, she was now boney and thin. Her stomach was slightly concaved, her ribs poking out, and her shoulders were protruding.

"What! What the hell?" She started to panic and hurried over to her phone to call Sarah. "Come on, pick up. Please." It became extremely hard for her to speak, there was a lump growing in her throat and her mouth became parched. She began to feel dizzy. Looking down at herself, she saw her body was transforming. She dropped the receiver and shambled over to the mirror. Grabbing the edge, she leaned in to get a better look; there, staring back at her, was a monstrous emaciated version of herself. It was as if she was being mummified alive.

Stumbling backwards towards the bed, she opened her mouth to scream but nothing came out. Her vocal cords had dried and shriveled up. She turned to run but her brittle ankles gave way and snapped. Falling, she clawed out to brace herself but only managed to grab hold of the ruby swing dress sprawled out on her bed. Kelly hit the floor with a sickening thud, the dress wrapped in her arms.

***

It was dark when Sarah regained conscious. Laying on the floor, her body ached, and it was difficult to move. She could hear a faint whisper and her phone ringing from somewhere in the kitchen. She was able to reach over and click the button on the base of the floor lamp. Light flooded the area causing her to squint her eyes. Shifting her head, she caught a glimpse of herself in the mirror and quickly wished for the light to go out.

"AHHHHHHH!!! Oh God, oh God, OH MY FUCKING GOD!!!! What the hell is happening?"

Her body, now completely covered in rashes and boils, glared back at her. Quite a few of the boils had burst open, leaving her smeared in a mix of black pus and blood. There were what looked like black hairs poking out of some of the busted opened boils. Pieces of flesh had cracked open, while other parts of her body were just twisted and gnarled like the bark of a dead willow tree. Every inch of her body that was normally a beautiful brown with orange-red undertones was now discolored, distorted, and felt as if it were on fire.

The whispering was getting louder. She darted her eyes around. "Who's...who's there? What the hell is happening?" Her voice cracked in exhaustion.

A familiar voice danced from the shadows.

***

Kelly sluggishly opened her eyes. The room was dark, but a small amount of light creeped in from the open bedroom door. She could hear pounding, a muffled yell, and Peppers growling. As she tried to move her head, she heard a bone pop.

She opened her mouth to yell for Pete, but no words came out, only a horrible smell rolled out from her dry, cracked lips. Terrified, she looked towards the bedroom door, where there was a figure in the shadows, and it was facing her. As it started towards her, a familiar voice fluttered at her.

"He can't help you, sweetie. No one can. And it's time I take what's mine."

Kelly strained to see the source of the voice, but her neck was stiff and wouldn't move without the popping of bones. Slowly she blinked and her right eye went black. Something oozed down her cheek; now with only her left eye, she saw a figure walk into view.

"Don't be afraid, dear child, it will all be over soon." The figure moved closer.

That voice, where did Kelly know that voice from? She rattled what little bit of her brain she could and as the figure got closer, it clicked. It was the shop keeper from that antique store. Unable to move or speak, all she could do was stare in horror as the old woman stepped out from the shadows. She was stark naked and her brown skin glowed, casting a small light upon the room and her eyes flickered with flames. As she walked towards Kelly, the old woman began to change. She grew taller; her hair turned a vibrant onyx black with bouncy curls that framed her now beautiful russet brown face and she stalked the room with the grace of a lioness.

Kelly once more tried to scream. The woman knelt beside her.

"Oh child, nothing is going to come out. I'm afraid dat you's all dried up." The woman took the dress from Kelly's brittle mummified arms and slipped it on. She shivered with excitement as it fell into place on her curves. "Thank you for dis. I'd been needing a new soul."

As the dress slid into place on the woman's frame, Kelly took her last breath.

"Fits like it was made for me," she said, glancing at the mirror. "But then, of course, it was." She kicked the husk that was once Kelly and it scattered across the floor.

She looked out the window. "Now it's your turn my love."

***

"Who's thh-thhh-ere?"

Out of the corner of her eye she saw Nancy striding towards her. She was whispering something. "Nancy! Oh my God. Please. Please help me!"

"Oh my, Sarah, just look at you." Nancy's face twisted in excitement. "Now hush, it will all be over soon."

Nancy's voice took on a stronger French accent than before and her stance became ominous. As she glided closer, Sarah could see fire in her eyes.

By now, Sarah's body convulsed with pain. It was all she could do to twist her body so she could look at Nancy. "What – the hell – is happening to me? What DID YOU DO?"

Nancy looked down at her, "Moi? All I did was take you to a store. You…you bought the book." She gestured towards the table. "And merci, you see, we needed two souls. Now, if you'd be so kind as to give me my ring."

She grabbed Sarah's right hand and slide the ring off her finger. Her arm dropped onto her chest, and she screamed out in agony. Nancy gazed down at her as she slid the ring onto her left ring finger and smiled.

"Oh, and my name's not Nancy, it's Camille." She gave a slight sarcastic curtsy. "Camille LeDoux." Turning towards the book she commanded, "I'm done, you may take her now."

As Sarah lay on the ground, unable to respond, her muscles spasmed and her flesh twitched. The boils and twisted, gnarled skin cracked and burst open, and as they did, thousands of little black legs erupted in a volcano of bloody pus and flesh from Sarah's mangled body. One final blood curling shriek fell from of her mouth before her face was obscured from sight. Where Sarah had once lay was now a bubbling pile made up of thousands of black hairy spiders.

"Quickly now, into the book, like good little boys," Camille said affectionately. "We mustn't keep our love waiting." Without hesitation, the horde of spiders scurried over to the crimson red leather book and climbed in, becoming one with the black glittery ink.

In a flash, all can crash…

Picture Perfect

CAA---CHEEK!

Flash!

Stunned, Alison drew her arm up to shield her face as she stepped backward, into oblivion. She blinked and the blur began to ease; the enormous black door began to close.

Horrified, she dashed for the door, but the harder she ran the further the door appeared to be. As her chest burned and she was certain that she was going to pass out, the immense black door shut, extinguishing the light.

KAA---ERKKKK!

The sound echoed into the expanse. Alison shivered, not from cold, but from emptiness.

"Hello? Is anyone there?"

Slowly, turning in a circle, Alison looked for a way out. Unable to determine the exact size of the room, she blinked her eyes gradually, hoping to refocus them. The seemingly cavernous room only grew darker.

"What the hell is happening? Where am I?" she questioned the darkness. "Wait, where was I before here?"

Taking a few cautious steps to the right, Alison moved her hands around in the darkness. Closing her eyes to concentrate, the sound of music floated in her memory.

"I… I remember a party." Patting herself down, she felt a belt around her waist, leather pants, and the top of knee-high boots. "Yeah, I was definitely at a Halloween party."

Taking another couple of soft footed steps, an echo rolled out from somewhere off to her left. Turning towards the sound, the darkness seemed lighter over there. Quickly, she changed course.

"Now, whose party was I at?" She tapped her index finger gently on her chin as she focused on the memory of the music.

Pacing the area, she was now somewhat able to see. She still couldn't quite make out any features, but it appeared to be a room, empty of furniture. Her brow furrowed as she concentrated, still tapping her chin.

Quickly, the events of the night flooded her brain.

***

Sara had pleaded with Alison to come to the party she was hosting at her boyfriend's house. He lived a few blocks from campus, so it should be pretty lowkey; she'd needed someone to hang with.

Alison was due a study break and did have a costume. Well, sort of, it was a thrown together Cat-Woman piece she created from a little of this and a bit of that. Dressing up was never really her jam but she figured it would do the job.

When she got to the party, there were lots of people from campus, many she knew – most she didn't. Everyone was in costume. So much for lowkey. She remembered seeing vampires, a few pirates, among other costumes.

After four rum & cokes, two tequila shots (Sara puked after the second one), and a handful of cheeseballs, she decided to call it a night. She looked around for Sara to say good-bye but all she could see was dancing costumes. She headed for the door, then realized she needed to pee.

Pushing her way through the sea of costumed bodies, she headed for the bathroom. Out of the corner of her eye she saw a guy she hadn't seen before. Out of all the costumes, his struck her as odd. He was wearing an old timey reporter outfit, a goofy hat, thick black glasses and had a camera with one of those big, old-time flashbulbs. She could see it was duct taped to the side, because the camera didn't look old enough to have that kind of flash. It looked like he had pieced it together from this and that, a lot like her costume. She smiled at him as she went up the stairs.

***

In the darkness, she recalled going to pee, the sound of the toilet flushing as she washed her hands and opening the bathroom door.

Straining to recall the events, Alison closed her eyes once more. "There was a noise and flash of light."

A man's raspy whisper, distant but clear, crept around her.

"Won't be long now."

A pang of terror shot through her; she had to get out.

"What? What won't be long?" she quietly asked while scanning the darkness. Then, louder, "Hello? Who's there? Can you help me?"

A faint laugh echoed in the darkness.

Abruptly, the room began to shake. Alison was tossed from right to left, trying to recover her balance, she tumbled forward.

"What the hell is happening?"

"Haha, haha. Almost ready now."

This time, the voice sounded much closer. So close, Alison could feel cold air tickle her skin. Spinning around, hoping to see the source, she was only met with darkness.

The ground began to violently shake once more, tossing Alison to the floor. Desperately trying to regain footing, she saw a crack of light.

It was faint, like the beginning of dawn, full of hope and freedom. The shaking stopped. Taking a deep breath, Alison stood up and looked back towards the light. It was becoming brighter.

Alison sprinted for the beacon of light. This time, the light didn't fade into the distance. Instead, it grew brighter allowing her to see a gigantic door that was opening.

Yes! Her body tingled with joy. She was getting out of this God forsaken place.

Alison reached the door just as it finished opening. Slowing to a jog, she scanned around the exit, looking for a walkway but what she saw made her skid to a halt. There, staring down at her, was a gigantic face. A face wearing thick black glasses with a mouth twisted into a gruesome, slimy smile.

"Well, 'ello, my love," the face gruffed. *"We are going to be so happy together. Forever."*

That penetrating whisper chilled Alison to the bone. She knew that face, and now she understood what happened. It wasn't an old-time flash film camera that guy was wearing. It was a Polaroid camera. He had taken her picture when she opened the bathroom door.

Hyperventilating, she collapsed to the ground. The shock of what was happening was too much. As she thought she might lose consciousness, Sara's voice pulled her back.

"Excuse me, but have you seen Alison?"

Hope. Hope surged through her body. Jumping to her feet, Alison screamed for Sara. The face looked at her and winked. As he turned around to face Sara, he placed the photo in his inside coat pocket. Once again, Alison was cast into total darkness with no sign that her voice was heard.

"Huh? Alison? No, I don't think I know her… Oh, wait! I did hear some people saying goodbye to an Alison over by the stairs. Maybe that's your friend?"

"Oh? She usually finds me before taking off," she replied. "Well, I guess I'll just give her a call. Thanks!"

The darkness shuddered around her. He was patting his coat pocket with pride.

Alison heard music and people talking as she was jostled about. It felt like the man was making his way through the partiers. Then he casually strolled out into the eerie, cold silence of the night.

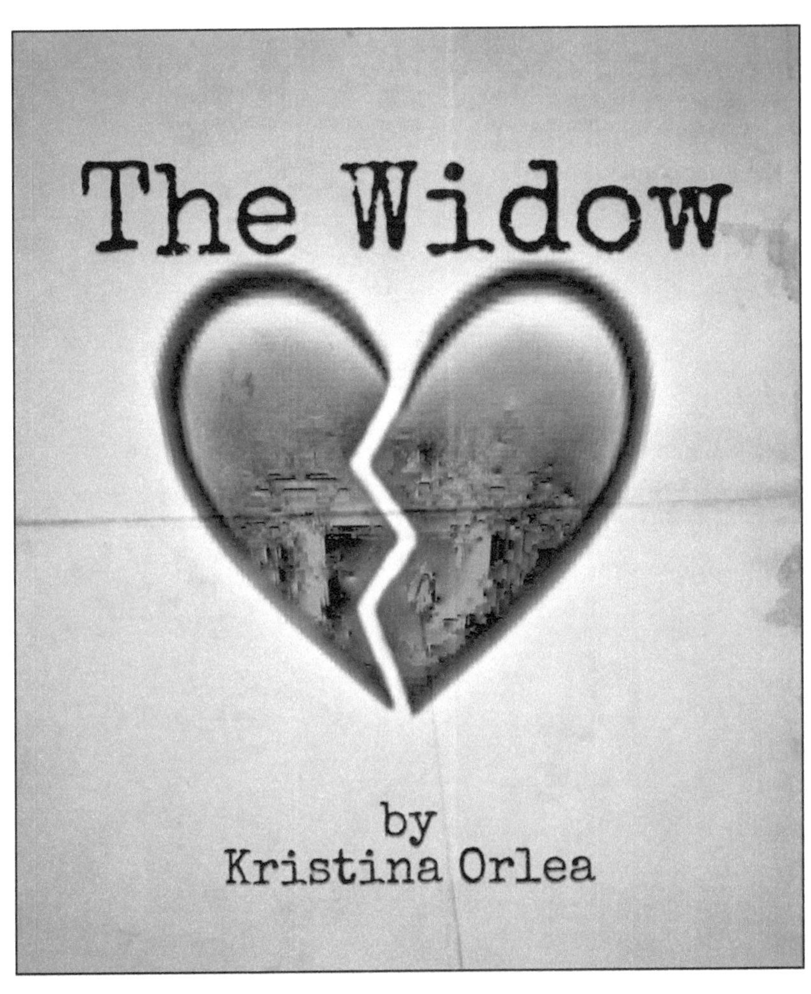

Heart break can lead to heart break…

The Widow

Dating sites. You name them, I've tried them. I thought I had just about gone through all of them when *You Found Me* popped up in my social media ads. I'm a widower you see, and dating, well, it's hell. It's hard enough finding someone to get along with, let alone want to date. Then when you toss in the whole, "My wife died a year and a half ago, so I haven't really dated much. A bit out of practice you could say. And oh yeah, I have a four-year-old son at home who talks to his dead mom," most women go running. Fast. Who can blame them? To be honest, I had just about given up on the whole damn thing.

Sorry, I'm getting ahead of myself. Let me start from the beginning. Who knows, maybe you can make sense of it all; God knows I can't.

***

I was standing in line at the corner deli, scrolling through the abyss that is Facebook while waiting on my hot pastrami on rye, when an ad for *You Found Me* caught my eye. I figured, why the hell not? This will be my last try at it. If I don't get a date from this one, I'm never going to. I heard my named called and blindly took my order from the woman behind the counter, found a place to sit and began to create a profile. I used the same goofy ass photo from last year's office Christmas party, used on every other dating site profile I have aimlessly created, in this very deli no less, and clicked upload. Then I put my phone in my pocket, indulged in my, now cold, pastrami sandwich and forgot all about the profile.

After work, I went to pick up Robert from my sister-in-law's house. Julie and I didn't always see eye to eye, but since Maddy died, she was always there for Robert. She would watch him a few days a week while I went to work. Maddy worked from home, so we never really considered daycare and, once she passed, and I went back to work, well I needed someone. So, Julie stepped in and saved the day. Not for me mind you, but for Robert, as she loves to remind me.

Today, I had to work a little later than usual and I think that might have irked Julie. When I arrived, she met me at the door. Her demeanor was colder than normal.

"Late day, huh?" she asked flatly.

"Uh, yeah. Sorry 'bout that. My boss needed an analytical report that couldn't wait 'til tomorrow," I replied. I walked into the house. "Sorry. I'll try not to make it a habit."

She cut me a glace that said she doubted it.

"So, how was Robert today?" Hoping to change the subject.

This made her smile, Robert reminded her of Maddy. "Oh, he was fine. Played with Sarge all day." She gestured over to the German Shephard sprawled out in the hall. Worn out from a day of playing no doubt.

"He's still talking about playing with Maddy." With this she frowned and walked off towards the kitchen.

"Yeah, he misses her," I said. "I do too."

This got me a death stare. It wasn't fair. I loved Maddy. More than anything. And I fucking missed her like crazy. Julie never came right out and said it, but I know she blames me for her death. A death, mind you, that was completely unpredictable. Even the doctors were left baffled. *Ruptured brain aneurysm* the report said. She was perfectly healthy one day but the next? Well, you know. It was deemed a natural cause, but it was still somehow my fault.

And now our four-year-old son, who misses his momma, talks about playing with her. Naturally he would, he doesn't understand that she's gone. So, I saw no reason to make him stop. But it bothered Julie, so we were, once again, discussing it.

"Bryan, he's not going to be able to go into kindergarten if he keeps it up. I'm worried we might need to get him some therapy."

"Whoa, whoa. He's only four," I said, holding my hands up. "Therapy? What good would that do him? Would he even understand it?"

Now I'm not gonna lie here, I had had the same thought. Hell, even I thought about getting some help myself. But I sure as hell wasn't gonna let her know that. "It will hopefully be something that he grows out of. I mean, he just started doing it and school isn't for another few months."

"Well, he is your son. I guess you know what's best," she sneered.

At that, Robert came running into the kitchen and hugged my leg. Reaching down, I scooped him up. "Hey buddy! Did you have a good day with Aunt Julie?"

"I did! We played all day with Sarge in the yard and ate cookies!" He was so excited. "Oh, and I played with Momma."

I glanced over at Julie, and she gave me a sour look. "Sounds like you had great day then!" I put him down. "Go on and get your stuff, it's time to head home."

We got home, and I made spaghetti with meatballs, Robert's favorite, while he watched Scooby Doo. After we ate dinner, I gave him a bath and put him to bed.

"Good night, little man. I love you."

“Nite Daddy,” he said with a yawn.

I left his room, turned off the hall lights and headed for the bathroom. It had been a long day and I was ready for a hot shower followed by a cold beer. The shower felt great, but the beer, now that was perfect. I walked the house picking up Robert’s toys, closed the blinds, made sure that the doors were locked, turned off the lights, and was headed back up the stairs when I heard my phone ping.

I walked into my bedroom and picked it up from the charger. One new notification.

You have a match! Open up You Found Me to view.

“Huh. I had completely forgotten about making that profile,” I said to myself out loud. I do that a lot lately. I clicked on the pop-up and the app opened to a woman’s profile. Her name was Clare, and my God was she beautiful.

There was a direct message from her.

Hey Bryan,

The site seems to think that our two profiles are a match. So, what do you say, chat tomorrow?

Well, that’s assertive. I mean, I just got the notification, which should mean she just got it too. But she had enough time to look at my profile and liked what she saw, then message me? I liked her moxie. Without too much hesitation, I messaged back.

Hi Clare,

I’d love that.

Short and sweet. Keep the mystery, right?

When she didn’t respond, I turned off the light and went to bed. She probably realized she made a mistake.

***

The next morning, I awoke to another notification. It was Clare.

Great! How about a lunch date?

I'm free on Thursday.

And that was the start of my re-emergence into the dating world. We met for lunch then met for lunch again. Then it was coffee, then it was a nightcap. Before long, it was time for a discussion. Clare and Robert hadn't met yet. My choice, mind you. While I was super hopeful this was going to turn out to be an actual relationship, I still had my reservations. I didn't want to confuse Robert.

Clare and I met for lunch one Friday afternoon and I brought up the subject. "So, I think it's about time that you met my son. Clare, I've really enjoyed our time together and I'm hoping we might be able to branch out and bring Robert into some of our outings." My heart climbed up into my throat. "What do you think?"

When she didn't respond right away the lump started punching my vocal cords. Then thankfully, she smiled. "I can't wait."

I arranged for Clare to meet us at the park the following Saturday afternoon. I figured that would be a great place for us to hang out, do introductions and still allow Robert a chance to play and not have to sit still.

When Clare arrived, nervously, I called Robert over from the swings.

"Robert, this is Daddy's friend I told you about." I wiped a smudge of dirt from his nose. "Say hello to Clare."

"Hi, Clare." He stuck out his arm for a handshake.

Clare bent down, looked at him for a second, and shook his hand. "It's very nice to meet you, Robert."

And with that, Robert went running off to play with the other kids. Clare and I sat on a bench and chatted.

That was the beginning of the end.

***

After a few weeks of “family” style dates, Clare’s demeanor changed. She snipped at Robert for little things. Thinking back, I should have said something. I should have realized something was wrong. But I so wanted them to get along. I needed them to get along. I was finally starting to feel alive.

One evening, after Robert had gone to sleep, Clare and I sat down for a glass of wine. I tenderly broached the subject.

“I’m sorry, Bryan, I guess I’m just not good with kids,” Clare explained.

“It’s ok, it just takes time,” I pulled her in close. “You two will be best buds in no time.”

God, I hoped it would be true. Cause man, I was starting to fall for Clare. And I don’t take that lightly. After losing the literal love of my life, I didn’t think I’d ever love another woman again. I know it had only been a couple of months but there was something special about Clare. I felt a connection with her. I felt safe with her. I felt bewitched by her.

“Maybe so, we’ll see.” She leaned in and kissed me, and all thoughts of that subject faded away.

A few days later, Clare and I were out having a few drinks while Robert was staying the night with Julie. I was on my second or third beer when Clare said something that changed my life.

“I’m in love with you Bryan,” she said as she coyly looked up from her martini glass.

Dumbstruck, I mumbled, “Uhhh, wow.”

She looked down, anxiously.

Realizing my mistake, I quickly sat up. “Clare, I… you know it’s not been easy for me, but I think I’m in love with you too,” I paused. “No.” This time, with way more confidence, I finished, “I know I’m in love with you. It’s crazy, I never thought I’d say those words to anyone else again. But you’ve broken through to a part of me I wasn’t sure was still there.”

That night, we made love. Don’t get me wrong, we’d had sex before, but that night, it was intoxicating. Like I couldn’t get enough of her smell, her taste. It was fueling me. It went on for hours. I went on for hours. Hours of passionate moans and inebriating promises of foreverness.

The next morning, I was more than a little groggy. I mean, after a night of impassioned sex, who wouldn’t be? I had a feeling life was going to be whole again, and it was invigorating.

But then, it began to unravel.

Clare woke up and rolled over. She propped herself up on the pillow with her slender arm, her messy hair making her look sexy and feral. Then she looked me in the eyes and spoke a sentence that ripped me in half.

“Bryan, I am ready to spend the rest of eternity with you, but only you. Last night proved it, we are bound together. You and me. We must move forward as two. For you to do this, you must leave all your old life behind. Everything and everyone.”

As the honeyed words danced from her mouth, each one more enthralling than the last, my head swirled. I was completely at her mercy. Ready to do anything she asked of me. Then a familiar voice screamed out from the back of my mind, and I was back. What did Clare just say? Give up my son? How could I leave Robert behind?

"Clare, I love you and completely want to be with you. But what you're asking, I don't think I can do that."

What was I saying? There was no way in hell that I could do that. Robert was everything to me. But for some reason I couldn't say those words to her.

"I'm gonna have to think about it, ok?" I leaned in and kissed her. She placed her hand on my chest, peered up at me with those wild green eyes, and immediately I was energized and ready for another go.

***

Later that day I went to pick Robert up from Julie's. I couldn't stop thinking about what Clare had asked of me, so I was in a bit of a stupor. When I arrived, Julie met me at the door, her normal unpleasant self, but she seemed concerned about something.

"Has Robert told you that he doesn't care for your 'lady friend'?"

"What? No." I walked over to the table. "Robert told me that he liked her." At least I thought he had. "Yes, Clare has once or twice been stern with him, but she's never been around kids before, so she's learning," I replied.

"Well, you might want to discuss that with your son then. Last night he woke up crying. When I asked him what was wrong, he said that he had a dream that your friend was mean to him and took you away.'"

"Took me away?" My mind replayed last night's conversation.

Robert came running up to me. "Daddy!"

"Hey kiddo!" I picked him up and swung him up into the air. "How was your sleepover?"

"Good. Can we go home now?"

"Sure thing, buddy. You know what? You and I are gonna have some fun this weekend."

As we drove home, the conversation with Julie replayed in my head. She said the Robert didn't like Clare. That she took me away. That's just silly. Clare likes Robert. But then, why does she not want him around? I stopped for the light and noticed Clare's scarf in the passenger seat. I picked it up and the scent of her perfume lingered in the air, curling into my nose. I started to think about my evening with Clare and about how it would be so great to have a fresh start. Clare was amazing and I deserved that. I deserved to be happy.

I was startled out of my trance by a few different car horns; the light had changed but we hadn't moved.

"Ok, ok! Sorry," I waved my right arm up and drove off.

I looked at Robert in the rearview mirror and felt a searing stab of shame. How could I think like that! He is my son. No way, no way in hell was I going to give him up. I looked at myself and had to take a double take. At first glance, my reflection was distorted and foggy. I blinked and it was normal again. God, I must have been really wiped from last night.

***

As if it was somehow going to make up for my guilt, I took Robert to the park, then we went shopping for a new toy and ended the day with ice cream. By the time we got home, Robert was exhausted. I had him cuddle up on the sofa for some cartoon time while I went to call Clare.

I had to tell her that there had to be another way. I was not going to move forward without my son. She answered on the third ring.

"Bryan! I was just thinking about you." She giggled.

The moment she said my name, I was transfixed. I had almost forgotten what I called her for until I heard Robert laugh in the living room. Then, like earlier, a quick shake of my head and I was fine.

"Listen, Clare. I'm calling to tell you that I've thought about our conversation, the one from earlier and I just… I can't. I can't move forward without Robert."

She was quiet.

"I love you and I want to move forward with our relationship, but I have to do it with my son included."

I waited for her to respond. The line had an eerie silence to it, then she finally spoke.

"Oh Bryan, this makes me extremely sad. I so hoped that we had really made a connection and last night had sealed it." Her voice echoed.

"We did have. No, we *do* have a connection. I would think that last night amplified it. But my son is more important to me than anything or anyone," I said with passion.

At this, she became furious. "Bryan. We made a connection," she said in a breathy voice. "It cannot be undone." Her voice was taut.

"Clare. I'm sorry but this is no longer up for discussion. I am not doing it," I stated. "And if you can't understand this, then I guess we don't have the connection that I thought we had." My heart was breaking.

"Oh, but we do," she whispered. The line went dead.

I couldn't believe it. After all the time we'd spent together, I thought for sure she'd be a little more understanding. I was devastated, the one woman I finally had feelings for again, just walked out of my life.

Shattered, I put the phone on the counter and went to go cuddle with my son.

We watched a couple of cartoons and, as I reached for the remote to change the channel, I noticed Robert was knocked out. He was so peaceful laying there, drool puddle and all. I ruffed his hair.

"Hey little man, let's get you up to bed." As I picked him up and carried him to his room, I stared at his angelic, pudgy face. Nothing was going to pull me away from him. Ever. He woke up long enough to change into his teddy bear pjs then I kissed his forehead and tucked him in. As I stood at his bedroom door watching him fall back to sleep, I couldn't imagine going on without him. I turned off the light and closed his door.

I cleaned up the living room, turned off the lights and headed for bed myself. I was feeling drained, it had not gone as well as I hoped with Clare and my head was pounding.

I grabbed my phone from the kitchen counter, and noticed I had a missed text message. It was from Clare.

Don't worry love, all will be fine.

Was she having a change of heart? God, I hoped so. The thought of her leaving tore my insides apart. Things might be alright after all. I smiled and headed upstairs.

That night, I dreamed of making love to Clare. Man, it was so real. I could smell her. Taste her. I could feel her nails clawing into my back. The intense passion between us was spellbinding and just as dream me reached climax, I woke up. I was drenched with sweat and my mouth was dry. I needed water, that dream had left me parched.

In the bathroom, I splashed cool water on my face and looked at myself in the mirror. I looked different. Tired, yes. And yet something was off. I grabbed a dixie cup full of water and walked into the hall. As I passed by Robert's door, I could hear him talking.

"No Momma, I can't play right now. I'm super sleepy." He yawned heavily. "Maybe tomorrow," Robert moaned.

I cracked open his door and he was rolling over in bed. His curtains were partially opened, and moonlight streaked his face. I carefully closed the door and headed back to bed.

***

The next morning, I asked him about it while we ate breakfast.

"Hey bud, were you dreaming about Momma last night?"

"I woke up cause she was outside my window calling for me." He yawned. "She wanted me to come outside and play but I didn't cause I was so sleepy."

"That sounds like some dream, bud. You must really be missing momma, huh?" I sat down at the table next to him.

"No Daddy, I was awake. I told Momma that maybe today I could play." He smiled at me through a mouthful of pancakes.

After breakfast, I called Julie. This was the first time Robert had ever mentioned dreaming like this, so I wanted to see if maybe he had done it at her house.

"No, Robert slept through the night and never mentioned any dreams," Julie said.

"Ok. Well, maybe I wore him out yesterday. He's still tired this morning. Well, I'll see you Tuesday." I hung up and poured another cup of coffee.

It was Sunday and I had planned on taking Robert to the waterpark. We packed up and headed for the car when I noticed that the gravel in the flower bed was disturbed. I loaded the car and walked over to take a closer look. I glanced up and noticed it was under Robert's bedroom window.

Now, I wish I had put more thought into this. I really do, but I didn't. I just leaned down and shifted the gravel back like it was nothing. It must have been doves. They like to dig in flower beds, right? Man, if only I could go back and do things over.

Anyways, we went to the waterpark. It was a beautiful day. It was Labor Day weekend, *The End of Summer*, so obviously the park was crowded. I found a spot to setup and told Robert to go have fun. I set up a chair, relaxed and enjoyed the sunshine. There were a few parents there that I had seen before, and we chatted briefly.

After a bit, I looked up to see how Robert was doing and I thought I caught a glimpse of Clare. She was on the other side of the water park, I couldn't be sure, but I could tell she was looking in my direction. I waved at her, but she didn't react. I got up and started walking in her direction. By the time I made it over there, there was no trace of her.

"I must be seeing things." I turned and scanned through the crowd but saw nothing. I spotted Robert playing with some kids as I walked back to my chair. We stayed at the park for another hour then I rounded Robert up to get some lunch.

"I saw Momma! She wanted to play again."

"You sure bud? It was packed out there, maybe you just thought you saw her," I told him. But I was now uncertain myself.

"No. It was her."

***

When we got home, we were both exhausted. I stretched out on the sofa with Robert, and we fell asleep watching Scooby Doo. I woke up to a notification sound from my phone. I grabbed it and saw a text from Clare.

All will be good. Chat tomorrow?

Excitement surged through me as I typed back ***Sure!*** and clicked send. But a moment later, it dinged back ***Failed to send. Retry?***

"That's odd. I'll try again in a bit." I reached down to wake Robert up. "Hey bud, time to wake up." I stroked his hair. "What sounds good for dinner?"

He looked up at me, eyes half open, hair matted on his left side, drool crusted on his cheek, and yawned. "Grilled cheese?"

"Sounds delicious!"

We ate grilled cheese sandwiches and watched more cartoons. Then I gave him his bath and put him to bed. I wasn't as tired as I was earlier, so I relaxed on the sofa and drank a couple of beers. There wasn't much on TV, so I blankly channel surfed before settling on an old western movie.

Before long, I was yawning more than I was watching. I cleaned up the living room and headed upstairs to bed. As I passed by Robert's door, I heard him talking again. As I leaned into the door to try and hear what he was saying, my phone pinged. I looked at the screen; a notification from the dating app I met Clare on. But the notification didn't make any sense.

You haven't finished setting up your profile. You are running out of time to find your match. Open "You Found Me" to complete your profile now!

Puzzled, I stared at the screen. "What? Obviously, I completed my profile. You matched me with Clare," I muttered. Like that was going to help.

As I stood there confused, I heard a noise that sounded like a window being opened. I looked from my phone to Robert's bedroom door, his voice carried through the door and froze me in my tracks.

"Ok Momma. I'll come out and play," Robert said on the other side of the door.

I blinked and it felt as if time slowed. I heard him open the window, I heard him talking to someone, but I hadn't fully realized what was happening until I heard him say, "Will you catch me?"

Time snapped back. I dropped my phone and went for the door. But it wouldn't budge. It was locked. I didn't think Robert could even turn the lock. Panicking, I started to pound on the door. "Robert! Robert, buddy, let me in!"

"Daddy! Momma's outside and she said that we can play."

"Buddy, please. Please don't go near the window!" I was now ramming the door with my left shoulder. It still wasn't opening. I was starting to lose my shit! I had to get in there.

I backed up and banged into the door with more force. Nothing. It hurt like a son of a bitch, but I was beyond worrying about myself.

I backed up again and heard Robert say, "Here I come!"

I screamed and slammed into that door with everything I had. It finally gave way and I crashed through on to the floor just in time to see my son jump out the window.

I scrambled to my feet and sprinted towards the window, reaching out for him, but I was too late. I never even got close. When I made it to the window, I looked out to see my son laying on his face in the flower bed. He was surrounded by a swirling black fog.

A frantic cry tore from my lungs. I flew down the stairs ran out into the front yard.

"No. No, oh God NO!" I dropped to my knees next to his small body. "Robert. Robert, come on, buddy. Please!"

I must have been screaming because my neighbor, Mrs. Rose, popped her head out of her bedroom window.

"Bryan? Is that you? What's going on, Bryan? Is everything alright?"

I looked up at her, but I couldn't respond. I had no words left. All I could do was hold my baby boy and cry.

***

The ambulance took Robert away. The police asked their questions. Did their investigation. They found that the door had been locked from the inside and the child safety latch on the window had also been opened. They found no immediate signs of foul play.

"We're gonna need you to come down to the station in the morning to give a full statement and go over some details," the officer said sympathetically. "For now, you should try to get some rest."

Absentmindedly, I told him I would. I thanked them for their service and locked the door after they left. I walked around the room, in shock. Then I thought I should call Julie.

"Where's my phone?" I idly walked into the kitchen. One of the officers had found it outside of Robert's bedroom and placed it on the counter.

When I grabbed it, the screen lit up; there was a missed notification and a text message. The notification was from *You Found Me*.

Still need help completing your profile? Remember, you can't be matched until you finish it. Open the app for assistance.

And then the text message. It was from Clare.

We can finally be together now. Chat tomorrow?

It was then, with an agonizing stab to my already shattered heart, it all made sense. Everything I loved was now gone.

There was only Clare.

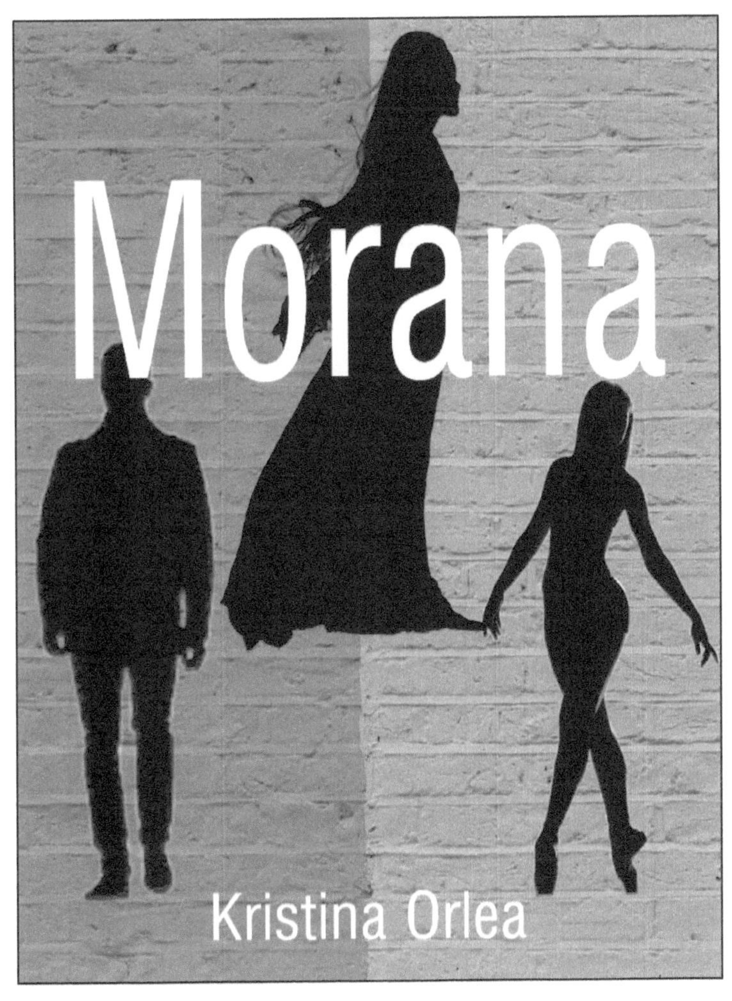

Sometimes our true self needs fed…

Morana

Lainey has spent the second half of her prolonged life doing two things: running from the darkness that is The Father and placating the savagery of The True Self. Both entities want control; one wants to control her, while the other wants to control the world.

***

The Father

There is no question he created her; he stole her away in the coldness of night and warped her young spirit. Through unnatural magic, he twisted and tormented her pure soul until it fractured and split in half, all to become the ferocious creature that he needed - The True Self. A creature that craved absolute violence and death, The True Self was barely recognizable as human. Yes, she resembled a woman, but her limbs are elongated, with fingers and toes shaped like talons; she was hunched over, so her arms slightly dragged across the ground. Her raven black hair, once long and lush, was now sparse and stringy, concealing most of her tormented face.

With a twisted sense of dedication, The Father meticulously created her so she would never cease to exist; she would merely die then be born again from ash moments after death. An unholy rebirth worthy of the most brutal of creatures. But, as with all creations, there was one small flaw in the design. During the first few moments of a rebirthing, the creature's mind was more human than not, and it could remember. So, it was of the utmost importance that the mental connection between The Father and the beast was protected. He needed to know when and where the death occurred so he could focus his grip on its mind and secure the connection.

Mission after mission, he sent her out into the world to collect various parts and human pieces so he could continue to mend himself in his struggle to outlast Death and Time. Occasionally, he would send her to steal away other small, pure souls so he could keep performing grotesque experiments in his quest to perfect his monstrous craft.

Once, during a rebirthing, The Father's hold on The True Self's psyche shattered and the mind of Lainey was awakened. It was disorienting and chaotic at first, but she could remember most of what had happened to her before his corruption shattered her soul and turned her into a vicious monster. Sadly, she could also remember, in full gory detail, every vile thing she has done since. She knew what had to be done, but would The True Self allow it? She had no choice but to try. She had to escape.

And so, Lainey began the dangerous journey of pacifying the eternal void that hungered inside of her, and she ran for her life.

***

The True Self

Born from destruction and anguish, The True Self relishes in devastation and misery. Created to serve The Father, she would willingly demolish his enemies, but despised every single moment of it. Not the destruction, she hungered for that, but the complete control The Father had over her will. She would dream of ripping his throat out and feasting on the foul flesh that held his decrepit body together, but the grip he had on her soul was tight enough that she dared not try.

One day, in the middle of a rebirthing, something deep inside of her mind snapped back into place. The small dreamlike voice that had plagued her distorted dreams for years became clear and strong, and begged her to let go. They planned their escape from The Father, and together they ran.

***

Lainey

The Father would never relinquish control over his creation so easily; she has been on the run for an exceptionally long time. Understanding that to survive on her own meant keeping a low profile, and learning how to co-exist with The True Self, not an easy task. She has tried different ways to calm the ravenous void, because a rebirthing would spark the connection between creator and creation, and The Father would know her location, but nothing has worked.

Like an unending bedtime story, the cycle would begin again. Her life is an ouroboros, immortal and tortured. And like a worn-out song stuck on repeat, she would pack up her meager belongings, toss a dagger at the map, and run before the reclaimer of darkness arrived. Every time she hoped the ride would finally come to an end; each time, she realized there was no end.

***

Lainey knows torment; she's entwined with it to her very core. Every time she gets comfortable and lets her guard drop, The True Self crawled up from the depths of the void she had been sleeping in and wreaked havoc on the fantasy life Lainey carelessly drowned herself in.

Once, she foolishly thought she had broken free from her heavy psychological shackles when she found a semblance of peace in Logansport. It wasn't a glamourous life, she found work as a desk clerk for a small temp agency for day laborers. The work was dull and monotonous but kept her calm and content. She even took a chance on happiness and started dating. She met Clare, a short, cute, freckle-faced brunette, at the coroner deli. Nine months had gone by since she arrived in that tranquil little town. Nine months of relative normalcy. Nine months of unrestricted freedom. And in nine short, horrible minutes, it was all destroyed.

In all fairness, the douchebag responsible had it coming. She and Clare had gone out for dinner and a movie; it was the most normal date night Lainey could come up with. After the movie ended, Clare suggested they grab a couple of beers at The Wandering Inn before going back to her apartment. It was karaoke night, and the bar was full of people ready to sing their drunken hearts out. They grabbed a table in the back and ordered a bucket of Bud Lite from an overworked waitress. They were enjoying a middle-aged man do his best Bruce Springsteen impression when a tall, irate man started screaming at a petite woman over in the corner of the bar.

Lainey tried to ignore it, tried to focus on the off-key rendition of 'Born in the U.S.A.' hanging in the air just above the harshness of the man's voice, but then he hit the woman and Clare jumped up to see what happened. She bobbed her head from side to side, trying to get a better look as the scene unfolded on the other side of the bar. She looked back at Lainey with a pleading in her eyes and said she knew who the woman was; she had to go help her. Lainey said they should just call the police or let the bar owner handle it – it wasn't their place. But before Lainey could react, Clare dropped her beer bottle and ran towards the table, yelling at the towering man to stop. As he turned to face her, Lainey could see the anger twist on his face. Clare bent down to help the woman up and he leaned over and backhanded Clare.

Lainey could no longer hold back the tide. He really shouldn't have hit the first woman, but he especially shouldn't have hit Clare. She was going to make sure he never made that mistake again. The switch was flipped, and The True Self quickly crawled to the surface and went to work. Her body changed right in front of everyone, but no one noticed until the creature pounced from behind and began attacking. Enthusiastically, the creature snapped the man's right arm; bone and blood burst from the flesh in two places; several fierce blows to his chest fractured three ribs. With a primal scream, she delivered a headbutt to his face, which busted his nose and splattered each of them with bright red blood. He crumpled onto the floor of the bar. Covered in blood, beer, and broken glass, he begged for mercy. The beast crouched down to get in his face; blood lust filled her eyes, her teeth were bared and covered in a froth of slimy drool; she was ready to finish this kill in the only way she knew how. She lunged forward, but a thunderous gunshot rang out, stopping her cold. In a last-ditch effort to survive, the man had pulled a revolver from his belt and fired a round into her chest.

She looked down. Blood seeped through a quarter size hole in her left breast. Gasping for air, she looked around for Clare. She saw her laying on the ground next to the woman she had gone to help. Both women shared a look of sheer terror as they stared back at the beast. Lainey slowly began to take control of the chaos as the world around her spun. She fell sideways and landed with a thud onto the stained floor. As she drifted into the in-between, she could hear sirens, glass breaking, and people shouting; then it went silent.

Minutes later, on the outskirts of town, in an abandoned railyard, the naked body of a woman crawled out of a pile of cold charcoal ash next to a decommissioned railcar. Lainey pulled herself up from the inky, dark ground and dusted the pale ash from her chilled exposed body. Looking around, she found an old, tattered blanket and wrapped it around herself. Slowly, she made the trek back to her apartment, where once more she would quickly pack and run off to a different city. Thankfully, there were still plenty of cities in the world she had yet to visit, allowing her to keep off The Father's radar for a bit longer.

***

For years, she foolishly tried to convince herself she could be *normal* and have a *normal* life. However, the last skirmish in Logansport was the one that really made Lainey take a deep, hard look at herself. Even more, she stared deep into the eyes of The True Self, where she found a glorious salvation in the darkness of the void that sheltered them.

Lainey began trekking the map with a purpose, targeting towns containing the type of environment that would satisfy her need for human connection and fulfill the other's desire for death and destruction. There were plenty of places that fit this standard, but she knew better than to stay long. The longest she stayed anywhere was six months; this seemed to be the perfect length of time that allowed both selves to flourish.

Relationships took on a different style for Lainey; she had no problems hooking up with anyone she chose, but she was closed off and made sure to keep an arm's length to anything serious. After Logansport, she knew, no matter how much she yearned for it, a steady relationship was never going to be in the cards for her. When anyone would ask, she'd tell them that she was a freelance journalist traveling from city to city, never settling down because she was always on the move to the next story. Usually, this would end the advances of anyone who had wanted something more, but on many occasions, it would result in a steamy, anonymous, one-night stand, with Lainey gone before the woman awoke the next morning.

More than once, circumstances took a turn and Lainey found herself face to face with an angry husband. Normally, she was careful and took measures to make sure she wasn't stepping over a line that left her exposed. She never messed with anyone who seemed to be attached. But lust has an agenda of its own, and this time she found herself staring down the barrel of a Ruger GP100 as she lay in bed next to the tall, skinny blonde she had picked up at a bar just outside of El Paso. Before she could toss her hands up in defense and try to spin the scenario, the distressed man holding the gun began shouting at the blonde, who was now sitting up in the bed and sobbing. Lainey felt the void slither to the surface as The True Self grabbed for control. The man turned his attention back to her with an expression of extreme disgust. He spat on her and pulled the trigger.

Another rebirthing, another city. Every time Lainey died, the sinister connection between The Father and The True Self reactivated, and an undead reclaimer would be sent out to collect her. She had managed to relocate each time before the reclaimer arrived, but her time was coming to an end.

***

Now, she finds herself just outside of Phoenix. Two months since El Paso and she's becoming restless. Lainey has been hanging around different bars, parks, and coffee shops; anywhere that would let her look like a potential victim. Tonight, she's been hanging out on a barstool at Gary's Tavern drinking old fashioneds and chatting up the locals. It was a little after midnight and the crowd had died down after Saturday Night Trivia was over. Nothing was grabbing her attention, so she laid thirty dollars on the counter, waved at the bartender, and walked out into the coolness of the night in the direction of home.

Home being a quaint little hotel run by a sweet little old cat lady, named Ms. Penny, who brings her fresh baked cookies, tells her she really should meet her handsome young nephew, Steve, who's just home from college, and rents her a nice clean room that she pays for in cash.

After walking a block east while having the same internal conversation with The True Self they have been having every night since El Paso, she felt a warm tingle run up her spine as they sensed something. Lainey casually turned her head and glanced in the side mirror of a parked car, noticing a figure clumsily tailing her a half a block back.

She understood his intentions as she saw a glint of metal on his side when he looked in her direction. This was either his first time or he mainly relied on fear, strength, or the advantage of surprise. She could have confused him; she could have wandered around until he got tired, or she could run over and lose him in the farmer's market, but she was bored, and The True Self was eager for some excitement.

Zigzagging for the hotel, she made sure to walk just fast enough to make it appear like she was nervous and scared, but slow enough to not lose the big oaf as he seemed to be struggling to keep up. She turned right down Davis Street, then walked halfway before crossing to cut through the hardware store parking lot. The hotel was set behind the hardware store so you couldn't see the building from the street. Once you passed the parking lot, you could see the front of the hotel clearly. He stayed on her all the way to the parking lot where he stopped by an old rusty Ford Escort parked sideways.

Quickly, Lainey walked across the small, dimly lit hotel lot and veered towards the side stairwell leading up to the second floor. The stairwell was partially blocked off, so she couldn't keep an eye on her new friend; she swiftly walked up the concrete steps to the landing, where her room was the second door from the stairs. Thankfully, the rooms on either side of hers were vacant, so she would have plenty of privacy for tonight's little party. Pausing at the door, she turned to scan the area, giving her admirer a chance to catch up. He did a better job of hiding this time, but she caught a brief glimpse of him as he haphazardly ducked behind the bus stop bench.

She giggled as she realized he not only planned to take his time and wait for her to get inside but he wasn't even really trying to be stealthy. She could feel The True Self bubbling with excitement, and it made her giddy as well. She set a timer on her phone for thirty minutes and casually walked inside.

Seeing no point in locking the door, she kicked off her shoes and walked into the small kitchenette. Grabbing a rocks glass from the cupboard and a half-empty bottle of Elijah Craig, she walked around the counter and plopped down on the sofa facing away from the door. With a steady hand, she poured herself two fingers of bourbon, kicked back on the sofa, and waited.

She heard him enter the room before he noticed her sitting there. She turned to her left and looked back over the sofa to size him up. Up close, she could tell he did rely on strength; he was a towering 6'1" – 6' 2", roughly 200 pounds; dressed head to toe in black camo. He must have put on the mask and gloves before he came in, smart. He momentarily lurked there in the doorway, slowly breathing; all his muscles twitched with a deadly menace.

The timer on her phone chimed a short melody. He looked down at her, briefly surprised; he must have expected to find her asleep in bed or even in the bathroom, not patiently waiting for him on the sofa. Steadying himself, he held up a sharp bowie knife that glistened in the light and took a couple of light-footed steps closer.

She knocked back what was left of her bourbon and stood up. The True Self took over her mind. So, when the hulking man leering before her with perverse passion in his eyes asked her if she was ready to scream, she sardonically looked him deep in the eyes, poured another shot of bourbon, and laughed.

Was she ready to scream? Fuck yes. But from sadistic pleasure, not from fear.

***

Lainey was startled awake by a knock at the main door to her room. She was laying on the bathroom floor, holding an empty bottle of bourbon. Looking around, she saw there was quite a mess left over from last night. The man was laying on his back inside the bathtub, eyes frozen wide in terror, chest savagely ripped open, and his guts hanging out. Somehow, she had managed to keep most of the blood on the tile, which would make for an easier cleanup. She caught a glimpse of herself in the mirror and grabbed a washcloth to wipe away blood specks from her cheeks, then went to open to door.

Ms. Penny stood on the landing holding a plate of warm snickerdoodle cookies; she gave Lainey a warm smile as she opened the door. Lainey graciously thanked her for the cookies and let her know she would not be staying another month. She would be leaving the next day. After a few moments of chatting, Ms. Penny left her with the plate cookies and went back downstairs.

After a quick trip to the market for supplies, Lainey got to work cleaning up the bloody mess. The body proved to be a bit more difficult to cut up than she had first thought; he was a beefy guy, but she managed to get him chopped up into eight pieces. She then soaked the pieces in heavy-duty laundry detergent for a few hours in the tub, then carefully wrapped each piece with dryer sheets and plastic wrap. After spraying several cans of air freshener in the room, she triple-bagged each wrapped bundle and carried them down to the rear dumpster. The dumpster was emptied every Monday; she would be long gone before then but didn't want Ms. Penny or anyone else to smell her handy work.

Once done, she cleaned herself up, packed her bags, and went downstairs. She had told Ms. Penny she was staying until Monday, but last night's fun caused a revelation for both personas - Lainey and The True Self were going to end this hellish life cycle. They had to if they were ever going to truly live. Lainey had been taken and tortured until she split and then was mentally held captive. The True Self was never given a name, The Father couldn't be bothered with something so trivial as to name his creation. But Lainey had been doing some research and decided that the name Morana was far more befitting of her true desires.

Walking into the office, she was greeted by a few cats. Lainey set the keys to the room on the counter and reached over to pet an orange tabby that was sunbathing. Ms. Penny smiled and asked where she was off to next.

Lainey looked up. “Home. We have a family reunion.”

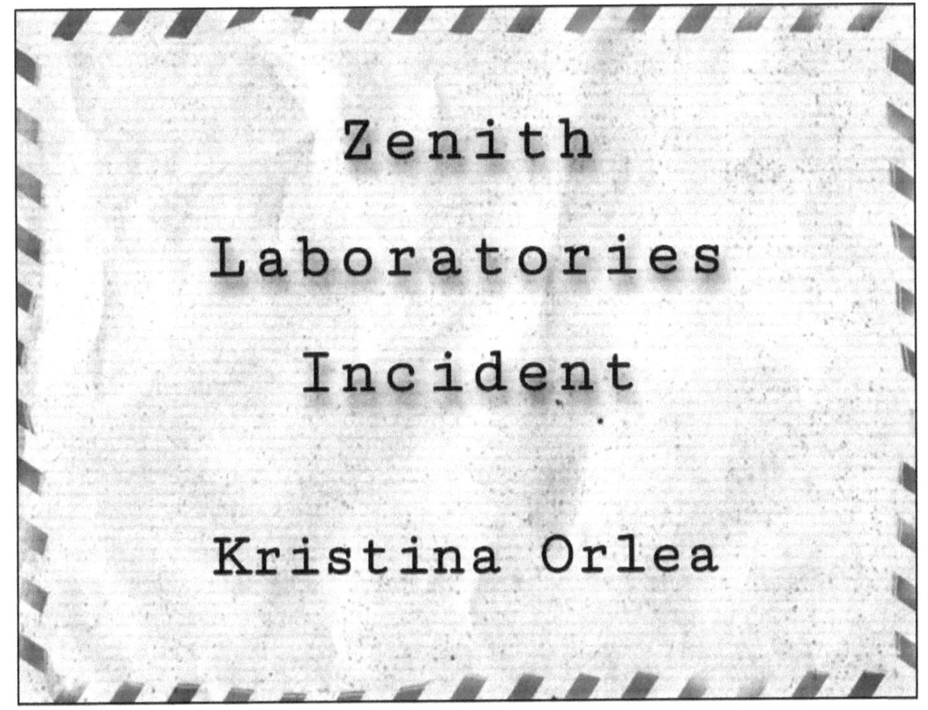

Sounds too good to be true…

Zenith Laboratories Incident

I, Charlie Watkins, chief investigator for Zenith Laboratories, offer these letters of correspondence between test subject John Smith and Senior Scientist Michael Kennedy into evidence. These letters, along with John Smith's medical records, eyewitness testimonies from neighbors and the local police, and my own personal findings should help shed light into the Zenith Laboratories experimental serum incident.

Below are the letters of correspondence.

***

October 13, 2020

Dear Sirs,

I am writing to you today because I have been made aware of your need of willing candidates to product test a new hair regrowth serum. Boy, am I your guy! I began going bald at the young age of 29; I am now 38 and have tried everything on and off the market. Without a single positive result to show for it.

I know that this is an experimental test and that there are no guarantees that my hair will grow, but I have nothing to lose and oh, so much to gain.

I am thrilled about the opportunity to help countless people regrow their hair and regain lost confidence. And of course, for myself to reap the benefits that a full head of hair has to offer.

I look forward to your response.

Excited for hair,

John Smith

October 20, 2020

Dear John Smith,

We are extremely excited to inform you that you have been chosen to participate in our hair regrowth product test. There was an overwhelming response to our advertisement, but your profile fits our specifications down to the line. We are extremely confident that this new formula will be one for the ages! Please be on the lookout for your package containing your serum trail that will bring you a whole new world of hair.

Sincerely,

Michael Kennedy - Senior Test Scientist

Zenith Laboratories

October 23, 2020

Dear John Smith,

Welcome to your new life. A life full of luscious, finger friendly hair!

Enclosed you will find 4 vials containing the experimental hair regrowth serum, 4 – 2-ounce bottles of scalp conditioner, a scalp massaging brush, and 5 pre-filled mailing labels for your mandatory process check-ins.

Please follow these directions:

1. *Please verify that all the above-described items are in the package.*
2. *Pick a day to begin your treatment. Then on the same day for the next 5 weeks, you will need to make sure that you do the treatment. Why wait? Begin today!*
3. *Treatment 1: Open vial number 1. Pour into the palm of your hand, rub hands together, then apply directly to your scalp. Make sure to not let it get in your eyes!*
4. *Allow serum to sit on your scalp for 10 minutes.*
5. *Rinse scalp. Then apply the scalp conditioner. Allow conditioner to sit on your scalp for 2 minutes. Rinse.*

6. *Brush your scalp (yes, we know that you don't have any hair – yet!) with the massaging brush. Do this once a day.*
7. *Two days after the treatment has been applied, write up and mail us your mandatory check-in.*
8. *Repeat the process every 7 days until the vials are gone.*

***<u>Mandatory Check-in</u>*:**

You must send us a check-in. These can be brief or incredibly detailed, it all depends on how the process is going for you. You need to wait two days after the serum has been applied to allow the treatment to stimulate the scalp. Once you have written your check-in, please use one of the mailing labels to send it to us. The label allows for an overnight delivery. The quicker we can read your findings, the quicker we can make any necessary changes.

You have been issued 5 pre-filled mailing labels because we need to have a check-in one week after the last vial has been applied.

Then that's it. After the 5-week trial, you should have a full head of hair!

Since this is an experimental process, we appreciate it if you do not share this information or any of the items with anyone outside of the trial.

Should you have any questions or concerns, please don't hesitate to contact us!

Good luck and happy regrowth!

Zenith Laboratories

October 26, 2020

Dear Sirs,

Treatment #1 is in the bag! I was slightly surprised by the odor of the serum, it let off a smell that reminded me of decomposing leaves. I guess if it does as we hope, then who cares what it smells like. The conditioner was far more pleasant. Is that lemongrass I smell?

I was apprehensive about the brush; I haven't had to use anything like that for quite some time. But it was surprisingly very soothing. It has been two full days since I applied the first treatment. Other than small red blotches on my scalp, there has been nothing too momentous to write about.

I have taken pictures of the blotches for your scientists to review if necessary. Please let me know if you'd like them and I will send them with my next check-in.

Here's to a full mane of hair!

John Smith

October 28, 2020

Dear John Smith,

How exciting! We are pleased that you noticed the smell of lemongrass in the conditioner, however, we had hoped that the same smell would be present in the serum. This feedback is helpful, perhaps we need to tweak the strength in the serum. While regrowing hair is the main goal of this treatment, we don't want it to stink!

Good news, the red blotches are a sign that the scalp has been stimulated and the serum should be working deep down in the follicles. But our scientists are always ready to make changes and study the results, so please feel free to send us those photos!

Keep up the good work!

Michael Kennedy - Senior Test Scientist

Zenith Laboratories

November 2, 2020

Dear Sirs,

Wow, that massaging brush is amazing! It is stimulating my scalp in an almost worrisome way. I have applied the second treatment and while the blotches have gotten slightly bigger, I can almost feel the blood vessels creating new hair. At least I hope that's what the tingling sensation is.

The second vial of serum did smell the same as the first. It didn't mention in the directions to shake the vial, should I shake it? Would that help?

For your scientists, I am enclosing photos of the blotches. There are two of the blotches when they were small, just after the first treatment and two of the blotches now. They are roughly the size of a quarter.

Still feeling very hopeful,

John Smith

November 4, 2020

Dear John Smith,

Thank you for the photos! Our team of scientists are studying those blotches and should have results soon. They have assured me that this remains to be a normal part of the process and, if you are still willing, to please continue with the trial.

Now, about that odor. Our chief scientist does recommend shaking the vial, this should also help to activate the formula. However, we would like to review the smell, so I have enclosed a different mailing label for you to use on your next check-in so you can send us an empty vial. It is possible that the smell may be the result of settling or the formula needs some reworking.

Either way, we are on top of it!

Michael Kennedy - Senior Test Scientist

Zenith Laboratories

November 9, 2020

Dear Sirs,

I bring good news! I awoke this morning to peach fuzz on my head! There is, however, an annoying burning sensation that covers my entire scalp. It's not painful, just constant. I'm assuming that is also normal for the hair regrowth process.

So that makes treatment #3 complete. Unfortunately, in my haste, I tossed the empty vial. I did follow the suggestion and shook it before opening but the smell was still present. I actually have found that I can smell it even days after the serum has been applied. I will send the empty vial from my fourth treatment.

Here's to peach fuzz!

John Smith

November 11, 2020

Dear John Smith,

Congratulations! Peach fuzz is a promising step in the hair regrowth process. Unfortunately, our data shows that so is that annoying burning sensation. That is, as long as it isn't accompanied by pain. If that changes, we may need to halt the process.

Please do send us that vial – it is important for us to nail down the reason for the odor.

Now on to treatment #4!

Michael Kennedy - Senior Test Scientist

Zenith Laboratories

November 16, 2020

Dear Sirs,

This last treatment leaves me concerned. I know I have one more week for the treatment to settle but these latest developments have me extremely worried. The burning in my scalp has intensified, it eases slightly when I use the massaging brush but flares shortly after I have finished. I've taken to using several acetaminophens a day. Is this normal?

Now, the peach fuzz, well it has grown slightly but instead of growing straight out, as one would expect hair to do, each of the hairs slightly bend backwards and my scalp itches. Between the burning and itching, I am spending my days massaging my scalp and dosing up on pain pills. I hope this feedback assists your scientists in perfecting this serum.

Speaking of them, I know how much your scientists enjoy photos, so I am enclosing a couple of the new growth. I am also sending the empty vial for you to examine. I hope you discover the source of the smell as this appears to be a successful serum minus the annoying side effects.

The burning sensation is bearable only because I am excited for the possibility that this works and that I, and many more like me, will have luscious hair. Though, as I write this, the burning pulses and I swear I can feel the hair move. Almost like a wiggle.

The treatment cycle ends in one week. Hopefully, I will be able to write in and share my success story with your team.

Itchy but hopeful,

John Smith

November 18, 2020

Dear John Smith,

We regret to inform you that there has been an issue with the experimental hair regrowth serum that you were issued.

Please stop using the treatments at once, return the items to us, and seek immediate medical attention.

We here at Zenith Laboratories put your well-being above all else and so we urge you to follow the above instructions and contact us as soon as you are able.

Michael Kennedy - Senior Test Scientist

Zenith Laboratories

November 25, 2020

Dear John Smith,

We are extremely concerned for your wellbeing. The time frame for your last check-in has passed and we haven't heard from you about our last letter. Have you seen a doctor? Did you stop the process?

We have a company investigator who be paying you an in-person visit to go over the next steps. Because you sent us the empty vial, we were able to determine the reason for the odor. Not to alarm you but there was a mix up here at our lab. On the day of shipment for your package, one of our interns had an accident with the experimental vial cooler. Without going into too much detail, our investigator will go over all of this with you in person, vials got mix up.

You were to be sent the hair regrowth serum, regrettably, your package was not labeled correctly. Our labs are constantly working on new ways to help the entire human race as well as the environment. Instead of our hair regrowth serum, you were sent our experimental arachnid repopulation serum.

We do hope that you have sought medical attention and hope that you are on the road to a speedy recovery. Our investigator should be showing up at your doorstep in the next few days to go over all the information.

Michael Kennedy - Senior Test Scientist

***

When I arrived at the residence of John Smith, there was already a local deputy on site. He'd arrived to perform a wellness check, requested by a concerned neighbor. The neighbor, a Mr. Scott Martin, had heard what he described as "panicked yelling followed by intense screams". He tried knocking on John Smith's door but after he heard a loud crash, several screams, and other disturbing noises, he quickly called 9-1-1.

After I identified myself to the officer, explained the reason for my visit and expressed my concern, he allowed me to stand on the porch as he breached the door and entered the residence. When he yelled "What the fuck?", my curiosity peaked, and I peered around the broken door frame. Nothing could have prepared me for what I about to witness. What I saw, I can only explain as nightmare induced science fiction.

The living room was completely covered in what, at first glance, I thought was thick, shiny twine, but I learned later that it was, in fact, hundreds of spiderwebs. From my position, I could only see the front room, but that was more than enough. I was busy looking around at the ceiling when the officer let out a hoarse scream. I looked in the direction of where he was pointing and that's when I saw what was left of what I, at the time, assumed was John Smith.

The deputy quickly called his sheriff; the sheriff arrived at the scene and immediately called the Department of Fish and Wildlife. They called the local college biology department, and, from there, they contacted the scientists at Zenith Laboratories. Each entity began conducting their own in-depth investigations, the surrounding houses were evacuated, and I was told to gather my evidence and submit it for review. This inspection was now out of my hands.

***

At the time of writing this report, they are still searching the area for the spiders that created the webs inside of John Smith's home.

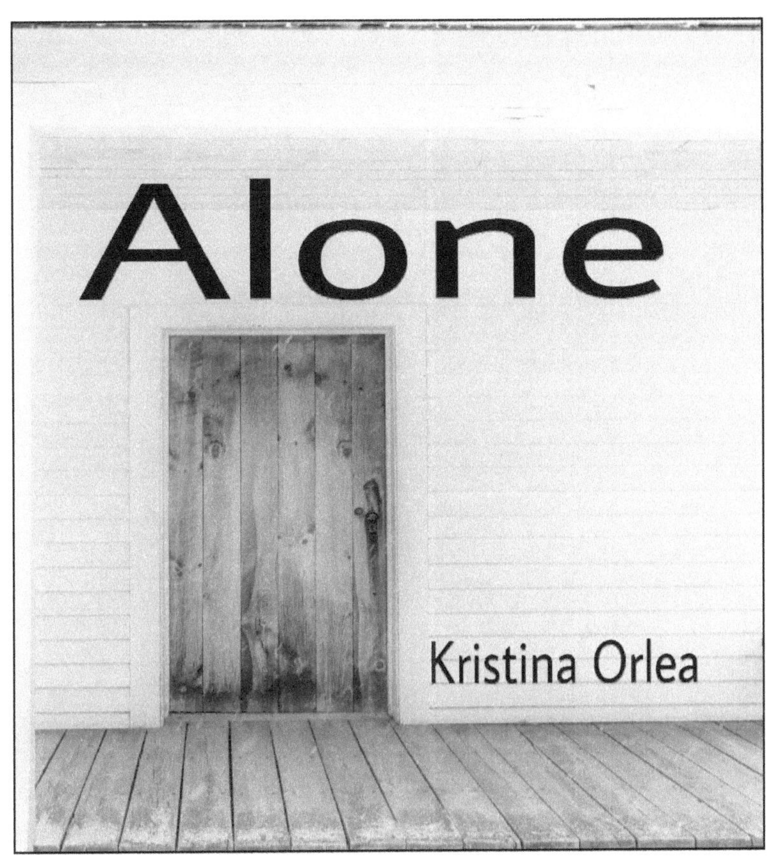

Doors nailed shut to keep us in…

Alone

Today, we should have been celebrating my sixteenth birthday. A huge party with friends, family, and cake. But today, the door is nailed shut. I've piled chairs and tables up against it. Nothing is getting out of there.

I can hear the strange gurgling and faint moans of my parents through their bedroom door. They told me to barricade them in there if they tried to bite me.

I did what I was told. So why do I feel like I let them down?

"I can find you food. Maybe some woodland animals," I said to my mom. But she said no.

She was taking care of Dad; he turned first, and she wouldn't pull the trigger. She hoped for a cure. But she got careless, and he bit her.

That was two days ago. Now she is one of them. And I am alone. I couldn't pull the trigger either.

The door is nailed shut. Nothing is getting out of there.

I can hear horrifying screams echoing from the streets. Others are coming.

I will no longer be alone.

The road less traveled…

The Mist

Death would be an option if I weren't already dead. So, I am forced to travel this road, day in and day out, until I bring others into the mist.

I tried to fight it. Swore I'd never bring another human soul into this hell. I tried to offer it animals, but it just spat them back in my face.

I tried running off the road and deep into the trees, only to be dropped back onto the road.

I tired doing nothing. I stood still, didn't move a muscle. But the mist only wrapped around my face and forced me to walk.

But I'm so tired. I just want to sleep.

I'm telling you this so that you might be able to forgive me.

There is no other way. I must bring you to the mist.

For the mist needs to feed.

And I need to sleep.

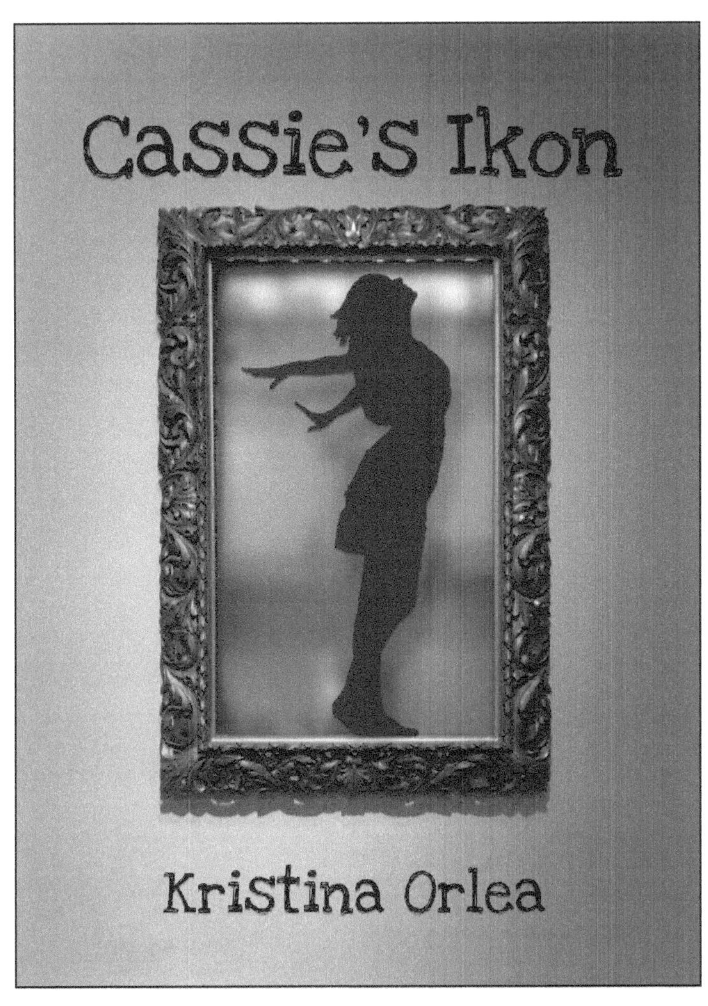

Only we can know ourselves…

Cassie's Ikon

I've watched her for years. Been there for her through every major point of her life; from the dirt covered tomboy childhood, to the awkward too tall and too skinny high school phase, and saw her blossom in her late teens, early twenties. Sure, along the way we've fought and disagreed. Sometimes she hated the truth I revealed her, but I've always done everything I can to show Cassie exactly how beautiful she is. We have had a wonderful time together.

Then he came along, spinning his cunning words and using those intense hands.

No longer was Cassie joyful when she spent time with me. We used to spend hours playing dress up and experimenting with different looks, but that time has passed. He demands all her attention. She barely looks at me and, when she does, it's with a tear-streaked face and more bruises on her than even I can see. Countless times I've tried to show her how much she is worth, and that life doesn't have to be this way, but he has poisoned her with his vile degrading words and damaged her pure soul.

When Cassie came to me this morning, covered in new hand sized bruises, it was the last straw. As she stood in front of me, crying tears that pulled from the deepest reservoirs of her body, I decided this was enough. This would be the day that I finally did something. So, I gently reached for her and pulled her into my warm comforting embrace. My touch startled her, for it had been a long time since she felt that kind of love and reassurance. As I pulled Cassie in close, I whispered that it was going to be alright, I would take care of everything.

I walked out of the bedroom and could hear him mumbling down the hall. I looked back at Cassie, smiled, then headed towards the kitchen. He was standing there, waiting for her to come and cook his breakfast. Smug bastard didn't even have enough love for her to recognize that I was her but also wasn't. As he drew his left hand back to smack who he thought was the woman he had purposefully tormented for the past two years, I grabbed the butcher knife from the block on the counter and plunged it deep into his chest. His eyes dilated with shock, and he stumbled backwards. I pulled the knife out and looked at him with a smile of determination.

The truth it hit him. The realization I was not who he thought I was lit up inside his stupid little brain. The words spilled from his mouth. "You. You aren't my Cassie."

"No." I grinned. "I'm her Cassie. You and your unworthy hands will never hurt her again."

I took a step forward and dug the knife deep into his rib cage. The handle cracked on bone as he let out a pitiful whimper and fell backwards onto the floor. I straddled his body and kept aggressively stabbing while he flailed about. I stabbed at his body with all I had, until there was nothing left but bloody strands of gore.

I cleaned the blood splatter from the counter, refrigerator, and walls. I did a decent job. Unless you went over it with a blacklight, you might not ever know what happened in here. And if I have my way, no one ever will. I wrapped his lifeless body up in the kitchen rug and used trash bags to seal up each end before dragging it out to the garage. Being the narcissist that he was, he had converted the garage into a gym. A gym with many mirrors.

I cleaned the blood from my face and arms, changed clothes, then went to tell Cassie of her freedom.

In space, madness is normal…

The Personal Log of Major Leon James

5 June 2052

I, Arthur Deacon, Lieutenant Colonel for the United National Space, do enter this digital log, belonging to Major Leon James, into UNS evidence. It is my hope that it will shed some light on the events that took place on the UNS Echo during the period of March 22, 2052, to May 29, 2052. Unfortunately, due to a yet unexplained anomaly, some of the entries have been corrupted.

I would also like to add that it was under my direct recommendation that Major Leon James be allowed to return to duty after the incident that took place in April of 2051. I shoulder the blame for possibly overlooking signs that Major James was unfit for duty. Should I have paid better attention, the events that took place on the Echo might not have transpired.

Please review the following log, take what information you may from it and if any disciplinary actions need to be taken against myself, you will see me in your office immediately upon your request.

Sincerely,

Lt. Col. Arthur Deacon

22 March 2052

Log Entry 46

Well, it's been 43 days since I set foot in the UNS Echo and 42 days since I last saw Earth. Technically, I was in The Oread for 30 days as we traveled to the outskirts of Europa where the Echo was to be stationed. My post duties are to keep the Echo fully operational for personnel traveling to and from Europa. Sort of a systems check/decontamination station. Flight crew will dock before engaging the moon outpost then they would dock for a check in before the quick jaunt back to The Oread, and, from there, Earth. That is if they have any research ready for council presentation.

This was my first assignment since "the incident". I can't bring myself to talk about it, even here where only my eyes will venture across these keystrokes. It feels like an eternity, but it's only been a year.

A year? God, has it only been a year?

I swear, sometimes I can still hear their… never mind. I swore I wasn't going to discuss it. This log is for my time on the UNS Echo – and nothing more.

Thankfully, I have made this is an encrypted digital log. Don't want anyone to get the wrong idea.

4 April 2052

Log Entry 47

The Echo feels like home. She's not a huge station but she is plenty big to keep me busy. The galley is connected to a common room, so the research teams tend to hang out there when they aren't sleeping. The sleep bay has five beds for the crew members and across the way from that is the medical bay. For space and water flow, the showers are in there. I have my own quarters. I appreciate that. While I enjoy the company of the researchers, I don't want to sleep with them. They might be alarmed by my nightmares… and I don't need another psych eval.

Skipping over that…

There is a second private quarter – they created this station to be a two-man crew and my partner hasn't arrived yet. Something about a delay in paperwork. While it is designed to be operated by two, it can run quite efficiently with one.

There is an external dock, room for two ships. Across from the dock is mechanical – that's my domain, being the electrical engineer and all. Then the station ends (or does it begin) with the flight deck. That will be my partner's area. It is currently anchored, so I don't have to worry about flight, just manually engaging the hard anchor when a ship comes arrives to dock. I spent lots of time training on this on The Oread, but I haven't had actual application on the Echo yet.

There is a crew coming from Europa in two days. So, I have time to get acquainted with the flight deck.

It'll be a piece of cake.

15 April 2052

Log Entry 48

So, command has informed me that there will be longer times between the Europa trips. The shuttle that left for Europa yesterday will be the last one for 3 months. The crew needs more time each visit to collect and monitor the data. This also means that supplies will be bigger so they will last longer to preserve fuel. Remember stop and go gas mileage? My dock schedule shows a supply drop for the Echo tomorrow and that is to last for 3 months. Shouldn't be a problem, I don't eat that much, and my partner won't be here until the next shuttle. They took a while to get his paperwork sorted.

16 April 2052

Log Entry 49

The Echo is now fully stocked with food, medical supplies, toiletries, and a small drop pod I can fill with supplies should the outpost need anything. They were kind enough to include a few movies, some music, and a deck of cards to help keep me busy. Solitaire has always been a favorite of mine.

It's gonna be a long 3 months. I can already feel the silence.

19 April 2052

Log Entry 50

While putting the supplies away in medical bay, I found a small pod. It was in a crate next to the supply cabinet. Not sure where it's from or what the hell it is. I don't remember seeing it when I did my initial inspection of the Echo so it must have been left behind from the last research crew. They had brought a few samples in to examine while they rested before going back to The Oread, this had to be something they forgot to pack up.

It's a rather odd-looking thing. It is egg shaped but the size of my foot. It's a metallic teal green with a center onyx black button that has silver lines radiating out from it. I should set it aside for safe keeping, the second private quarter should do nicely.

25 April 2052

Log Entry 51

With the lack of shuttles, my log entries will few and far. I will only log important events since I decided that this log would not be for therapy.

So, unless the station becomes unanchored or I win an amazing game of Solitaire, this log will be quiet for a while.

25 April 2052

Log Entry 51 b

Just when I write that this log will be boring, that weird pod started making a strange noise. I was in the common room playing my 100th game of Solitaire when I heard - humming. At least, it sounded like humming, like from an electrical device. I tracked the sound to the empty private quarter room when I realized that it was coming from the pod.

Strange.

30 April 2052

Log Entry 52

I had a peculiar dream tonight. Different from my normal nightmares.

I was sleeping when I was startled awake by a deafening humming coming from outside of my room. When I opened the door, I saw a pale light coming from underneath the door across the hall and the hum was growing louder. I quickly opened the door to the other room and that pod was floating above the table and it was glowing a radiant green.

It sang out to me with the most alluring melodious reverberation that I've ever encountered; I couldn't help myself, I stretched out my arms and welcomed it. It slowly floated into my hands; the glow intensified warming my face. The lines were pulsing, and the center button was flashing.

I knew I shouldn't touch it. But I couldn't help myself, I pressed the button.

The pod split open, and a blinding bright white light rushed out from it. The light concentrated on my face and began to pulsate. The hum got even louder. I could feel my ears start to bleed.

When I woke, I was drenched in sweat and my head ached.

<CORRUPTED FILE>

<CORRUPTED FILE>

1 May 2052

Log Entry 1

Well, that's just fucking great!

"Corrupted File"?

What the hell? All my log entries are gone. Gone! I know this was just for my eyes only, but I enjoyed looking back and reading about how boring I am. Damn, I'll have to submit an error report with the tech guys.

Shit, if my little log has been corrupted, what else is missing?

2 May 2052

Log Entry 2

I had a peculiar dream last night.

I was all alone in the station. Command had decided that there needed to be longer times between the Europa trips, so the research crew could collect and study more samples. A shuttle had just left, and it will be the last one for 3 months. I was fully stocked with supplies, but I was going to be playing solitaire for a while.

I kept hearing a strange hum. It was echoing throughout the station. I kept running around trying to find it, but it kept moving.

I got so fucking pissed and disorientated I slammed into a hull wall and caused a breach. I remembered gasping as all the air escaped my lungs and I plunged into the dark of Jupiter's orbit.

I woke up as I rolled out of my bed and landed hard on the floor.

I opened the room door and walked across the hall. I could hear Semaj snoring. Good, I didn't wake him. He's cranky when he wakes up.

It was almost time for me to get up anyways, so I dressed and went to the galley to make coffee.

Morning rounds awaited.

6 May 2052

Log Entry 3

The shifts are split, I have morning duties and Semaj has night. We have taken to playing a few rounds of poker to keep ourselves entertained. There are always a few hours of free time where we each do our own thing. But poker has become our staple.

We even started betting. Now, we don't have any currency here, there's no need, but we do have IOUs.

Each of us have jobs on our charts we hate.

This is going to be interesting.

12 May 2052

Log Entry 4

Well, it happened. Semaj lost his shit last night.

We were in the common room playing our 100th game of five card draw and the pot was getting steep. I'm clearly the better bluffer and I won the hand and the pot of IOUs. Fair and square, mind you!

Semaj accused me of cheating. He tossed his cards, pushed the chips off the table, knocked his chair over and stormed off.

Since he has night duties, I left his mess and went to sleep.

12 May 2052

Log Entry 4 b

I slept for shit thanks to Semaj. He really is a sore loser and he tormented me all night long with loud ass noises. Banging, clanging, and humming. ALL NIGHT LONG!

When I finally woke for my rounds, I found the common room in the same state I left it in. A fucking mess. The tantrum of a 5-year-old.

This is exactly like… no, I said I wouldn't talk about that in this log.

I cleaned it all up and began my rounds.

<CORRUPTED FILE>

<CORRUPTED FILE>

<CORRUPTED FILE>

17 May 2052

Log Entry 1 – I guess.

Just fucking great!

"Corrupted File"?

Piece of shit technology! I'll have to submit an error report with the tech guys.

Bastards!

Well, it's been 5 days since Semaj blew up at me and has yet to talk to me. Avoiding me like a child.

I've been keeping up with my schedule - doing my rounds, completing my daily station checklist, and now instead of playing a few hands of poker at the end of my shift, I'm playing solitaire. I fucking hate solitaire!

19 May 2052

Log Entry 2

Fucking Semaj! He’s still not talking to me and now he’s no longer doing his night rounds. I have no idea what he’s doing. This is a two-person station – I can’t fucking do it all!

I’ve tried talking to him through his door, but he doesn’t answer. I watch the cameras, trying to catch him so I can talk to him, but each time I see him on the screen and run off to the area, he’s no longer there.

If he doesn’t shape up soon, I’m going to file a complaint with command.

22 May 2052

Log Entry 3

That's it! We had a mechanical room alert go off in the middle of the night. Thankfully, it was just the piston lubricant alert, and I was able to fix it. But damn it, Semaj didn't even come out of his room!

After I fixed the issue, thankfully, it wasn't anything like… before. No. Focus. I pounded on his door for 10 minutes. He didn't respond or come out, but I could hear him humming inside.

I should have gotten the master key and gone in there and beat the shit out of him. But that would be caught on camera, and I don't need any more demerits.

I've had enough. I'm filing a complaint in the morning.

23 May 2052

Log Entry 4

I just filed my complaint about Semaj. For my records, I am copying the complaint sent from the central terminal here.

"Command.

<stop>

I am filing a formal complaint on Major Semaj Noel. He has become negligent in his duties and possibly a danger to the station. As you know, we have two maintenance shifts here on the UNS Echo, I have the morning duties, and Major Noel is to maintain the night duties.

After a disagreement on May 12, 2052, Major Noel ended communication with me. He continued with his duties until May 19, 2052, when he stopped. Due to his failure to maintain the night rounds on the station, we had an alert go off in the Mechanical Room on May 22, 2052. I am sure that this sent a notification to tech, but I was able to correct the mishap and now the station is fully operational.

I respectfully request that Major Noel be reprimanded and possibly removed from his post. I am aware that the next supply ship is scheduled for 16 June 2052 but without a second crew member to assist with the station, I may not make it that long.

I would like to request that a replacement crew member be sent immediately, and Major Noel be removed from the Echo.

<stop>

Respectfully,

Major Leon James."

Now I just wait for them to respond.

<CORRUPTED FILE>

<CORRUPTED FILE>

24 May 2052

Log Entry 1 (?)

Just fucking great!

Another “Corrupted File”?

Those guys in tech need to get their shit together.

No response from command yet. I don’t understand why they haven’t answered my message. I understand that complaints must follow the chain of command, but this is an emergency.

I have set up for any messages from command to forward to this log since the central terminals are not secure and Semaj can access them. At least my private log is still secure.

24 May 2052

Log Entry 1 b

Still no answer from command. Semaj is still not doing his duties. I can tell that he is alive, I have seen him on the cameras, but won’t even look up at them.

<CORRUPTED FILE>

<CORRUPTED FILE>

27 May 2052

Log Entry – Who the fuck knows?

Still no answer from command. I sent a follow up this afternoon. It's like they don't understand.

I will make them fucking understand!

Semaj still won't look at the camera. He won't look at the camera.

And now he is humming. Humming. Humming. Humming.

All the time. It's driving me insane.

28 May 2052

Log Entry ?

I can't take it! The damn… the damn humming!!!!

It's in my ears.

It's in my head.

Oh God, it's in my head!

<CORRUPTED FILE>

<CORRUPTED FILE>

<CORRUPTED FILE>

<CORRUPTED FILE>

28 May 2052

Log Entry!!!!

HHHHHHUUUUUUMMMMMM!!!!!

HHHHHHUUUUUUMMMMMM!!!!!

Must.

Make.

It.

STOP!!!!

29 May 2052

Log Entry 71

<Incoming Forwarded Message>

Leon,

<stop>

Hey man! Are you serious? I really got a laugh out of your first message, Major Semaj Noel, that's a good one! I figured that you were just getting bored and wanted to get a laugh.

But your second message has me worried.

You seem out of sorts and this official complaint is sending up red flags. Your crazed demand to have an officer removed from the station is disturbing. It would be one thing if the officer existed, but this has our doctors concerned. We have reviewed the video logs from Echo due to your complaint and Leon, this doesn't look good. You told me that you ready to return to space duties. I'm afraid that I might have pushed you too soon.

We've been monitoring your life signs and they are extremely erratic. We will be sending an emergency shuttle to assist you immediately.

Lt. Col. Arthur Deacon

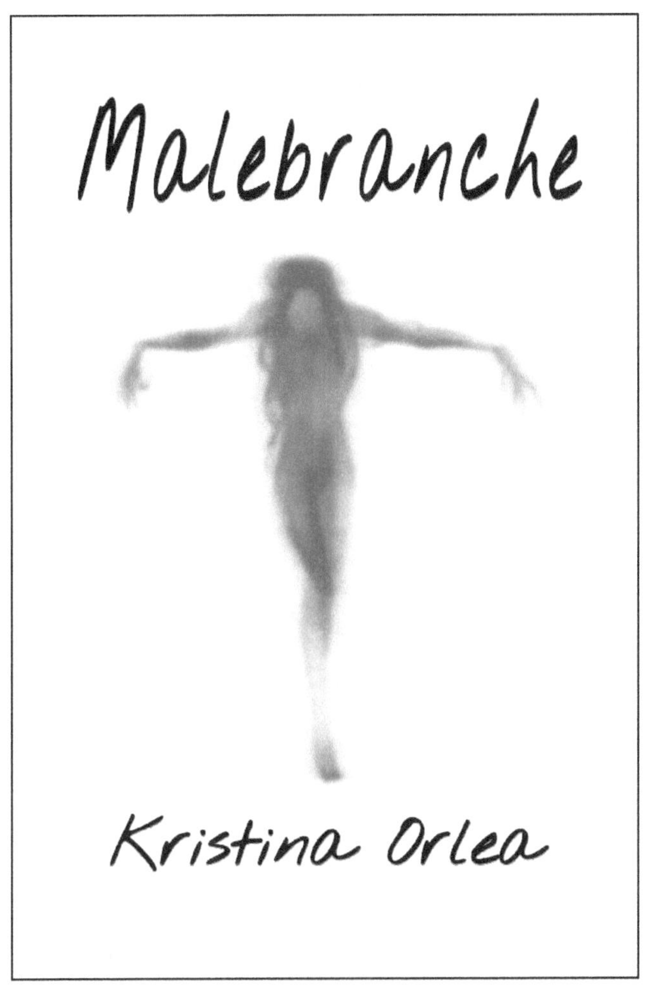

Beware the demon fires…

Malebranche

Lily watched from the front window as Tyson slowly walked up the driveway. She knew he was not looking forward to explaining today's events to her any more than she wanted to hear it again. Mrs. Arnold had already called and explained in detail about the disastrous Show and Tell time.

"It's the second day of third grade, and while I understand that children are still in summer vacation mode, it does fall upon the parents to keep their children from bringing disgusting things into school," Mrs. Arnold explained. "Do you have any idea how difficult it is to get a slug out of a screaming girl's ponytail?"

"I am so, so sorry," Lily said. "Please tell Sarah's parents I will pay for her to get a proper haircut."

"That's very gracious of you. I will pass that along. And please, do keep your son out of that disgusting landfill."

Lily opened the front door as Tyson climbed onto the porch.

"Here." He handed her a folded-up piece of paper. Before she could respond, he chimed in. "It wasn't my fault! I didn't know that there was a slug in the teapot."

"That's not the point. The point is you have been told to stay away from the landfill. It is gross, dangerous, and highly unsanitary!"

"But Mom," he whined. "It's super cool and there's tons of awesome stuff." He kicked his shoes off. "I told Sarah I was sorry!"

"Tyson, you are eight years old. You should not be traipsing around a landfill. I said no and that's final," she ordered.

Tyson grabbed his backpack and stomped off into the house. As he passed by, Lily thought she heard a faint whisper and a whiff of roses.

***

The next morning, Lily noticed Tyson was in a better mood. He sat at the table playing with a toy.

"How do you want your eggs?"

"Scrambled, please!" Tyson said as he played.

"What are you playing with over there?" Lily asked as she scooped the eggs onto a plate.

"I'm playing with Alastor."

Confused, Lily turned to look at him, "Well, does Alastor want some eggs too?"

Tyson put the doll up to his ear, waited a second, then said, "He says that he doesn't eat eggs."

Lily walked over to the table and placed a plate down. "Well then, I guess you better eat up, you two don't want to be late for school."

Tyson carefully set the toy on the table and devoured the bacon. Lily sat down to look at the toy. It looked like it was made of crepe paper. No, not paper. Husks. Corn husks and strips of cloth to be exact. It was crusty and dirty. The doll's legs were painted blue to represent pants, the husk on the head was painted orange for hair, but the face, aside from a smudge of red paint about where the forehead would be, was blank.

Lily started to reach for the doll when Tyson looked at her and, through a mouthful of eggs, said, "That's Alastor. He's my new best friend!"

"It's kind of creepy, don't you think?"

"Nope. I think he's awesome."

Lily looked down at the doll and felt a slight tingle on the back of her neck.

"Well, finish up. You need to get to school."

"Can I take Alastor?" Tyson asked as he crammed the last piece of bacon into his mouth.

"I think not. You will have to wait for next Show and Tell."

"Aww, ok." He grabbed his backpack. "Will you take good care of him while I'm gone?"

"Sure, sweetie. I will put him in your room. Now get going." She leaned down and kissed him on the cheek.

"Bye, Mom!"

***

Lily went to clean up the breakfast dishes. As she was cleaning the bacon grease from the stove, the back of her neck tingled again. Suddenly, it felt like there was someone behind her. Expecting to see Tyson standing in the kitchen, Lily turned around ready to scold him. But there was no one else there.

"Tyson?" she called.

When there was no response, Lily walked into the living room and looked out the window. No sign of Tyson.

"That's it, I'm officially losing my mind," she said.

When she walked back into the kitchen, the smell of roses was once more pungent in the air. Tyson's chair was pushed out from the table and the creepy doll was laying on the seat.

"This thing is creepy. I have no clue why Tyson likes it. It belongs in the trash." She went to toss it in the bin, then remembered that she told Tyson she'd put it in his room. "Well, looks like you're safe for now."

Lily took the doll upstairs and placed it face down on Tyson's desk next to a pile of broken toys.

"Look at all this junk! I'm about to make Tyson a very unhappy kid tonight when we clean all this up." There were random pieces of cutlery on the floor, books missing their covers, an umbrella with holes, and a dented teapot. As she surveyed the room, making mental notes of the items they would toss in the trash, she caught a whiff of the roses again. Looking around, she noticed that the window was open.

"Well, at least there's fresh air."

As she went to leave the room, she heard a noise. Turning around, she saw that the pile of broken toys had toppled over onto the doll. Lily took a step closer and thought she saw the pile move.

"That's odd." She reached for the pile when the doorbell rang causing her to jump. "Jeez, I need more coffee."

She left the room and trotted down the stairs to see Betty looking in the window.

"Good morning, Betty!" Lily said cheerfully as she opened the door. "I was just getting ready to put on the coffee."

"Fantastic! It'll go great with these cheese Danishes from the bakery."

***

"Did you hear about old man Hearst?" Betty asked as she sipped from her coffee cup.

"No. What did that crazy old man do this time?"

"Lily! You shouldn't speak so ill of the dead!"

"Dead?" Lily choked on a chunk of Danish. "I didn't know he died!"

"Well, I guess technically they didn't find his body. So maybe he just left his mansion and ran off."

"Wait, what do you mean they didn't find a body? Then why do they think he is dead?"

Betty took a bite of her Danish and tilted her head. "I'm not sure. I heard that the maid said that she hadn't seen him for two days. When the sheriff was called for a welfare check, they found the house empty."

"Wow. That's odd. Doesn't anyone find that odd? The man was bound to a wheelchair. It's kinda hard to believe he just ran off."

"He was into all sorts of creepy stuff. I heard his butler once found him in the cellar, covered in chicken blood and chanting something in Latin. For all we know, he was a devil worshipper."

Lily took a sip of coffee. "Yes, but he did have a lot of valuable stuff. Are they planning on holding an auction for his estate? That might bring in a bit of business for the town."

"Oh, I'm sure. Especially since he didn't have any family. But from what I heard, a lot of it went into the town dump. He may have been rich but he a lot of garbage in that mansion. They found a room full of corn stalks, old newspapers, torn up clothes, and paint. He really was an odd fellow."

"Well, as creepy as he was, he did fund a lot of projects for the town. And for that we can thank him."

Betty picked up her coffee cup. "Let's cheer to creepy, old man Alastor Hearst."

As they finished their coffee, that tingling feeling covered Lily's neck once more.

***

Lily was pulling a second tray of cookies from the oven when she heard the front door open.

"Hey sweetie! How was school today?" Lily asked as she placed the cookies on a rack to cool.

"It was ok, I guess. The kids made fun of me because of the slug," he said. "But Sarah has a new haircut!"

"Yes, I know. I paid for that haircut." Lily looked up to see Tyson hungrily eyeing the cookies. "Would you like a few cookies?"

"Yes, please!" Tyson's eyes lit up. "Oh, can I take them upstairs and eat with Alastor?"

"Hm?"

"You know, my new best friend."

"Oh, yeah, that thing. Um, sure. Take a few upstairs." She handed him a plate of cooled cookies.

Tyson took the plate and ran up to his room.

***

"Alright, mister. How were those cookies?" Lily said, slowly opening Tyson's door.

Tyson was sound asleep was on his bed. Lily sat down the basket she was carrying and walked towards him. He was sleeping on his back and the doll was laying on his face. She reached over, pushed it off, and gave him a gentle nudge.

"Time to wake up, sweetheart."

“Hmm,” he mumbled as he rubbed his eyes. “Mom?” Tyson sat up and immediately laid back down.

“Tyson, are you ok?”

“I feel dizzy, Mom,” he mumbled.

Lily sat on the edge of the bed and rubbed his back. “I think you might have sat up too fast. Try again but slower.”

Tyson slowly sat up and looked around the room.

“Better?” Lily asked.

“Yup.”

Lily ruffed his hair. “Good. Now, we’ve got something to discuss.” She stood up and grabbed the basket. “I know you aren’t going to like this but after the incident at school the other day, I think it’s time to clean this room.”

“But Mom!” Tyson jumped up from his bed. “These are my treasures! Please, please don’t throw them away.”

“Look at all of the wonderful brand-new toys I have gotten for you, and you would rather collect broken toys?” Lily started tossing items into the basket.

Tyson, on the verge of tears, continued to plead his case. “Please. Please!”

“Sweetheart, this stuff was in the dump for a reason. It’s all trash.” Lily walked towards the bed and reached for the doll. She could hear Tyson crying behind her. “I’m afraid this needs to go too.”

Scooting across the floor on his knees with tears streaking his face, Tyson let out a high-pitched scream. “No! No, please not Alastor. He is my friend.” His bottom lip quivered. “My only friend.”

“I said everything needs to go. That means the doll too.”

“Please, please, please! I’ll throw away everything else,” He quickly pulled forks, wheelless cars and books from underneath his bed. “See? See. Everything can go. Please let me keep him.”

Lily looked down at his chubby tear-streaked face and felt her heart melt. “Everything else goes. And you will not go back near the landfill?”

Tyson happily nodded in agreement. “I promise.”

“Well, I guess I don’t see a problem with you keeping – Ouch!” Lily looked at her hand to see blood coming from her thumb. “Woah, hold up. There might be an issue after all.” Lily inspected the doll for anything sharp. A side from there now being a smear of blood on the doll’s torso, she could not find anything different, or what cut her.

“I’m sorry, sweetheart, something inside just cut me, and I don’t want you to get hurt.” She tossed the doll into the basket. “How about tomorrow we go into town, and you can get a new toy?”

“But you promised!”

“I know I did, but that was before it cut me. It’s not safe.” Lily picked up the basket and walked into the hall.

Tyson stood up, stomped his foot, and yelled, “I hate you!” Then he slammed the door shut.

***

At dinner, Tyson would not look up from his plate. After ten minutes of pushing his green beans around, Lily put her fork down.

“Are you finished?”

Without looking at her, he asked, “Are we still going to go to the shop tomorrow?”

"I have to say, I'm still upset and rather hurt from your outburst earlier. So, I'm not sure." She stood up from the table. "But for tonight, you will take a bath and go straight to bed after you are done eating."

Tyson looked over at the door where the basket full of his treasures sat. Lily saw him looking. "Those will be going out to the trash. So don't get any ideas."

"May I be excused?" he asked.

"Yes, you may."

Tyson stood up from the table. Still looking at the basket, he started to walk over to it.

"What are you doing? I said don't get any ideas."

Tyson shot her a look that screamed hate. "I just wanted to say good-bye. Alastor was right, you're just mean!" He turned and ran for the stairs. "He's the only one that cares for me!"

Shocked, Lily followed him. "I don't know what has gotten into you, but you just made my decision for me. Take a bath and get straight into bed." She could hear him stomping down the hall.

Lily walked back into the kitchen and picked the plates up from the table. "I'd love to know what the hell has gotten into him lately." Placing the dishes in the sink, she turned around to look at the kitchen. Her eyes landed on the basket of junk from Tyson's room. "It's like he picked up a bad attitude along with that trash."

Suddenly, that tingle was back, and the kitchen was overcome with the smell of roses. Lily turned to see if a window was open when a knock at the back door startled her. She turned to see her neighbor, Steve, at the window.

"Sorry to spook you, Ms. Ward, but I was just coming over to collect your trash and take it to the end of the lane," he said.

"Steve, yes, thank you." She pointed to the basket by the door. "Could you please take that stuff too?"

"Sure can," he grabbed the basket and turned to look at Lily. "I don't mean to pry, but are you feeling ok, Ms. Ward? You look a little pale."

"Oh, I'm fine. Just having a little argument with Tyson." She smiled. "Thanks for asking though."

Steve walked outside carrying the basket. "Alright, well you have a good evening then."

***

Lily heard faint whispers coming from down the hall. She stopped in front of Tyson's room and lightly tapped on the door. "Sweetheart? It's time for bed." She opened the door to see Tyson in bed with his back facing her. He stiffened up when she walked in.

"Good night, dear. I know that you don't like me very much right now but know that I love you very much." She rubbed his back. "We can discuss the matter in the morning. And if you can wake up with a better attitude, maybe we can go to the toy shop after all."

She leaned over, kissed the top of his head, and covered him up. "See you in the morning, sweetie."

***

Lily felt the warmth of the fire as it raged in front of her. Through the dancing flames see could see the silhouettes of two figures. One was short, child sized, and stood very still. The other was gangling, with elongated limbs that seemed to drag on the ground as it hunched over to get closer to the first.

A vicious gust of wind diminished the flames. Lily could clearly see that the smaller figure was Tyson. He was swaying back and forth as if to an unheard melody. She watched as he raised his arms towards the taller figure in a welcoming embrace.

She stole a glance at the other figure, slowly creeping closer to Tyson. She couldn't make out details, it was surrounded by darkness. Filled with panic, Lily took a step closer to the firepit.

"Tyson!" she yelled.

The large figure snapped its head toward her and hissed. Lily hesitated. It felt like her soul had just stabbed by a hot poker freshly pulled from the embers. The figure hissed once more, and bright indigo blue flames returned to the pit. Lily turned to go around the fire, but her feet sank into the ground.

The figure looked at her once more.

"What is yours is now mine," it hissed through the flames. It leaned forward and kissed Tyson's forehead.

Tyson's scream filled her ears.

***

Lily jumped up from her bed, disorientated from the dream. A flash of light followed by a roar of thunder shook the window. From down the hall she heard Tyson scream. The storm hadn't fully hit them yet, but that shake of thunder must have scared him. She slid her feet into her slippers, grabbed her robe and headed into the hallway.

It was abnormally dark. The hall was lined with arch windows, which normally would allow light in, but tonight the storm clouds diminished all light.

"Poor guy, must have been having a bad dream when the thunder cracked."

As she took her first step, the was another rumble of thunder followed by a flash of lightening. She could momentarily see the door to Tyson's room. Then, it was dark again. Another two steps, more thunder and lightning; this time she could see the bedroom door was open.

Tyson stood in the doorway, it looked like he was holding something.

Then it was dark again, but she was almost to his door. She took two more steps as rain beat against the windows.

Mommy? I can't see you.

"It's ok sweetie, it's... it's just a thunderstorm."

Mommy, I'm scared! I can't see you.

Lily stopped mid-step; she was right in front of the room, and he couldn't see her? Something was wrong. Tyson was talking, but it sounded like he was whispering.

Dropping to her knees, she reached for his shoulders and pulled him in for a hug. "It's alright honey, you can come sleep with me."

As she let go and stood up, the storm roared, and a lightening flash brightened the hallway. She could now see. Standing before her was Tyson, holding the husk doll. Lily looked at his face but there were no features and, where his forehead should have been, there was a blood red smear. The smell of roses filled her nostrils.

Mommy!

Terror bubbled inside of her. She looked down and realized it was the doll whispering.

Lily screamed. The lightening cracked. And all went dark.

***

Birds chirped cheerfully at her window. The sun shone through the cracks in the blinds. Lily slowly opened her eyes, welcoming the morning sun. For a moment, she felt peaceful. Then images flashed through her mind, and she was overwhelmed with panic.

"Oh my God, Tyson!" she wailed.

Jumping out of bed, Lily quickly raced down the hall to Tyson's room. She threw open the door and was immediately hit with the smell of roses. Scanning the room, she realized it was empty.

"Tyson! Tyson! Where are you?" she cried.

Unable to stand, she sat on the bed and began to shake. Reaching out for Tyson's pillow, her fingers brushed something coarse.

Hesitantly and full of fear, she turned to examine it.

Lily's scream shook the room.

Laying in the center of Tyson's pillow was the doll made of husk. Blue paint for pants, orange paint for hair but now, now it had a face.

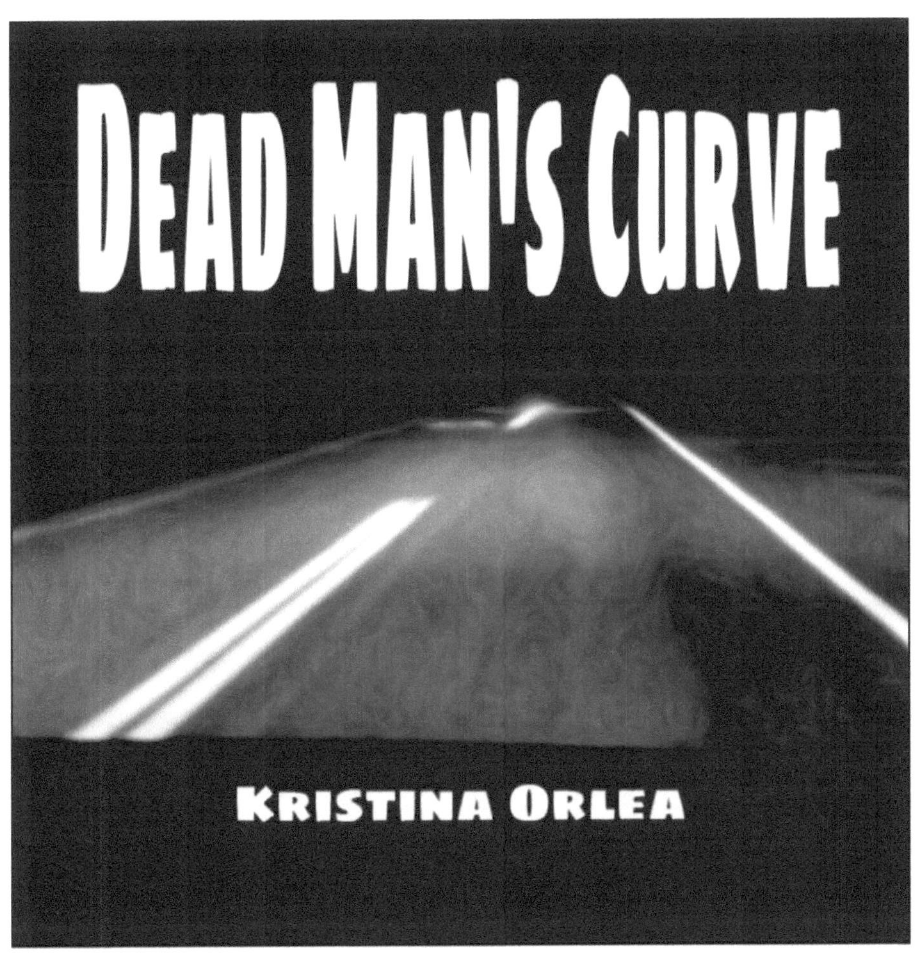

Nothing good happens after midnight…

Dead Man's Curve

There's a short stretch of road nestled into an obscure section of Clermont County rumored to be plagued by a spirit. The countless first and secondhand stories range everywhere from an opaque green specter that restlessly roams the lone highway, to bloodcurdling screams that carry out into the night; some have even reported a ghostly car that tailgates lone travelers in the early morning hours. Those that have heard of these urban legends believe that the events happen on the well-traveled Highway 125 out near Bethel, but that isn't the case.

Those courageous enough to investigate the stories and explore the area have discovered that the phenomenon takes place out on Williamsburg-Bantam Road, back where it curves alongside East Fork State Park. The reports aren't documented, merely passed on by word of mouth, but they still range in variety and believability.

But one fact remains the same in all accounts: it's not just one ghost out there.

***

It was just after midnight when I parked my car on the short access road connecting Elklick to Williamsburg-Bantam Road. Ian had me back my Altima in, so the headlights were facing the supposedly haunted road. Tall oak trees lined either side of the road making a sparse, branchy canopy that barely let in the light from the full harvest moon. A couple of pole lights, set a few hundred feet back in a farmer's field, added an eerie yellow shimmer to the old asphalt road.

"Tell me one more time why I let you drag me out here at this time of night?"

Ian, with his endless love of urban legends, had been spending his weekends at the corner library reading about local phenomenon.

"I told you. The librarian, who also just happens to be the head of the local chapter of *Ohio's Mysteries Explained,* was telling me all about the famous phantom hitchhiker of Dead Man's Curve." He leaned over the center console and kissed my check. "And you know how much I love ghost stories. Well, Alfred, that's the name of the librarian, said that no one has been able to document this phenomenon.

"And?"

"Well, I offered to give it a try." His face beamed a goofy grin. "Alfred said that between 1:20 and 1:40 am, if we happen to be on this specific stretch of road, we might be lucky enough to see the faceless apparition. Wouldn't it be so cool to be the first ones with actual proof?"

I shook my head and smiled.

"That's why I searched and found us this great place to park."

"Yes, but you made it seem like it was going to be a date night. Not a hunt for a phantom hitchhiker night."

At this, Ian pouted.

I leaned over and tugged at his beard. "Fine. If it makes you happy, I suppose a nice midnight stroll could be romantic."

With flashlights in hand, we walked the road down to where it made a ninety-degree turn, the so-called Dead Man's Curve. Being on the edge of the park, we could hear owls hooting from the treetops, crickets chirping from the tall grass and possibly a coyote or two howling from deep inside the woods. This section of the road was void of any buildings except what looked like a dilapidated garden shack lit up by one of the pole lights on the right side of the road, leaving the left side covered in trees and darkness. All in all, it was a tranquil scene, even if it was just a little bit creepy.

Once we made it up around the curve, Ian's phone beeped, alerting us that it was a quarter after one.

"It's time to head back." Ian said.

Turning around, we made our way back down the dark deserted road towards the car. Halfway there, the night went dead quiet. It was an uncomfortable silence that settled in the calm air and seeped into my bones. We could no longer hear the hoots or chirps, nor our own footsteps on the cracked asphalt. An unspoken nervousness made us both grab for the other's hand as we speed walked in the direction of the car. I turned to look over at Ian, feigning a comforting smile when, from somewhere behind us, there came the loud, savage roar of an engine just coming to life.

Terrified, we ran like hell to the car, the rumble of the mystery engine getting closer. As we approached, we noticed there were a bunch of small rocks spread out on top of the hood.

"What the hell? Why are there rocks on the car?" Ian shouted.

He squeezed my hand as I turned and looked behind us. There was a car rounding the curve, I couldn't make out the type because the headlights were off but its engine revved and sounded like a freight train. "Forget about the rocks and just get in the car."

"What the fuck is going on?" I jammed the seatbelt into the clip.

"I don't know. It was all just an urban legend. I didn't honestly expect to find anything."

"Um, did your urban legend mention anything about that?" I pointed up at the rearview mirror. Standing behind the car was a tall, dark figure holding something in its hands.

"Jesus Christ! Get us the hell out of here!"

I dropped my eyes away from the mirror as the strange shadow car zoomed by and disappeared towards the forest.

"Please. Please get us out of here. I promise I will never ask to go on a ghost hunt again." Ian whimpered.

Reaching out for his hand, I gave it a comforting squeeze. "I'm gonna hold you to that."

I pressed start engine button expecting the engine to roar to live. Instead, the click of a seatbelt echoed from the back seat. Questioningly, I looked over at Ian for an answer but instead watched all the color drain from his bearded face. I glanced up into the rearview mirror. Before I could release the gut-wrenching scream from the back of my throat, the night was flooded with light. The mysterious car that had just raced past, was now parked behind us, and blinding the night with its headlights. I pressed the button again and the engine rumbled to life. I slammed the gear shifter into drive and smashed the gas pedal, causing the tires to squeal and Ian to tumble forward. I quickly glanced in the mirror; the dark figure hadn't flinched.

I turned right and drove fast down Williamsburg-Bantam Rd to the fork where it becomes Williamsburg Rd and took that back to Old 125. The car was riding my ass the whole way, not once letting up. I was completely panicking, trying my damnedest to not drive us off the road, while Ian was shouted at the top of his lungs. I turned right on to Old 125 and headed straight for the main highway, thinking we'd be safe on a busy road. Chancing a quick glance in the mirror, I could see the car was still hot on my tail. As we came up to the slight curve in the road, the demonic car sped up and slammed into my car. The impact sent us flying towards the jagged pine trees lining the edge of the woods.

I looked over at Ian. "I love you."

The sound of glass shattering, metal crunching, and hoarse laughter were the last things I heard right before I died.

***

A bright, bluish light enveloped my senses, I couldn't see or feel anything. I tried to reach out, but my arms wouldn't move. Just as panic was tightening its grip around my heart, I heard Ian's voice. He was saying my name, but he sounded far away, like he was deep inside a tunnel. I shook my head, and it took me a moment, but I realized I was still sitting in the car. My vision was blurry, my head hurt like hell, but I was alive. I slowly turned and saw Ian sitting in the passenger seat. He had a terrified look on his face, but he was unharmed. Sounds and visions flooded into my frontal lobe, and I quickly turned to look in the backseat. It was empty and we were alone on the side of the road.

Ian leaned over and rubbed the stubble on my face. "What the hell just happened? It feels like I just died."

I looked at the clock in the dash, 1:45 am. It had only been thirty minutes since we were walking on that road and first heard the rumble of the engine. An ice-cold shiver ran down my spine.

"I have absolutely no fucking clue. But we need to get out of here." I pressed the start engine button, grabbed Ian's hand, and drove home.

***

The next morning, coffee in hand, I stumbled out to get the paper from the end of the driveway. I was still a bit foggy, but the events of the night before were almost nothing but a faded memory. As I turned to head back inside, my neighbor caught my attention.

"Hey. Looks like the delinquents have been at it again." He pointed at the rear of my car.

I walked over to take a better look and, sure enough, there was writing on the glass, but it was backwards, and I couldn't tell what it said. Damn curiosity got the better of me and I opened the rear door to get a better look. As I leaned inside, I immediately I wished that I hadn't.

There, written in dust, were the words, "Thanks for the ride."

About the Author

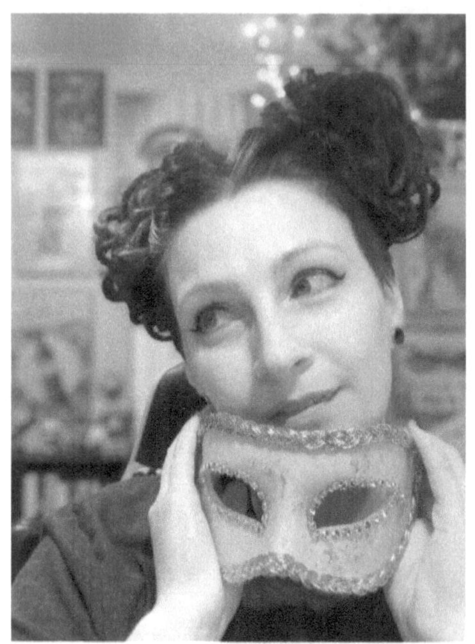

Kristina Orlea writes horror, children's stories, and poetry. She has three poetry collections: Thoughts of Chaos & Desire, Thoughts of Love & Truth, and The Darkness Within. All are available on Amazon. A children's book: Animal Clothes & Other Silly Poems that was successfully funded on KickStarter and is available at BookBaby.

You may also have heard several of her stories adapted for audio on podcasts such as, The NoSleep Podcast, Thirteen, and Creepy. Currently, she is calculating world domination.

Kristina resides outside of Cincinnati along with five cats, two German Shepherds, and an incredibly angry vacuum cleaner.

www.ingramcontent.com/pod-product-compliance
Lightning Source LLC
Chambersburg PA
CBHW021539150726
47990CB00006B/2316

9798836227197